THE PROMISE

JEAN ORAM

The Promise
Prequel: Book 0 (Veils and Vows)
By Jean Oram

© 2017 Jean Oram
All Rights Reserved
First Edition

Printed in the United States of America unless otherwise stated on the last page of this book. Published by Oram Productions Alberta, Canada.

COMPLETE LIBRARY OF CONGRESS CATALOGING-IN-PUBLICATION DATA AVAILABLE ONLINE

Oram, Jean.

The Promise / Jean Oram.—1st. ed.

p. cm.

ISBN 978-1-928198-79-6, 978-1-928198-40-6 (paperback)

Ebook ISBN 978-1-928198-32-1

First Oram Productions Edition: May 2020

ACKNOWLEDGMENTS

Thank you to Sarah Albertson for filling me in on the Canada vs. United States university differences including "hell week" and American exam schedules. Thanks for your help and good luck with your marking!

As well, I'd like to thank readers Donna W. and Mrs. X. for their help with reading through an early version of this book and providing feedback. And even before that, thanks to Lucy M. for your endless patience while chatting again and again about Olivia and Devon as I rewrote and rewrote. I hope my readers fall in love with the well-known Blueberry Springs hero Devon in a whole new way after reading *The Promise*. As well, special thanks to Rachel B. for pointing out inconsistencies and to Margaret for her fabulous edits to help make my sentences flow much more betterer. (That was a grammar, joke by the way!) And finally, for the proofing final touches, thanks to Erin D. and Emily K.

XO,

Jean Oram

A Note from Jean on The Promise...

In many of the Blueberry Springs books Devon Mattson was simply Mandy's brother, a character in the background making wisecracks. Then I wrote him as Nicola's best friend in *Tequila and Candy Drops* and I (along with many readers) fell in love with him. He was fun, strong, slightly wild, but also caring and sensitive, too. A wonderful hero—even if he didn't know what kind of ice cream to buy a woman who'd just broken up with the love of her life!

So, I decided to write a book for Devon—*The Surprise Wedding*. But it turned out Devon had this big messy past that had left him gun-shy about relationships. In figuring out his story, I realized that he really needed a short story to explain it all. The short story would help me write *The Surprise Wedding*, and as a bonus I could give that short story to my newsletter subscribers.

Then I discovered Devon had much more to say about his first love (and university/college days) than would fit into a teensy, couple page story. It was actually pretty big, and what I thought would take me a week took me several long months as I wrote and rewrote Devon's novella, *The Promise*. The book that now starts the Veils and Vows series.

On a more personal note, I was similar to Devon and Olivia in that I fell in love with The One during my university days—and got married just before my final year. (Getting married while in school was something I had told myself I would never do.) In writing Olivia, Devon's girlfriend, I had fun revisiting the freedom of those days as well as that scary, exciting feeling of falling in love with someone truly irreplaceable—all while trying to figure out who I was exactly. (Not that I have a perfect handle on that even now—I keep changing!)

But one of the best parts was getting to develop Olivia's feelings of empowerment and breaking down her hesitation in the face of Devon's confident 'just do it' attitude. I truly believe that when you find the right person, they help you grow and heal old wounds while challenging you to stretch, be strong and follow your dreams. Because of that, it was difficult writing the ending for these two lovers in *The Promise* because their ending wasn't what I wanted for them. *But* in their full-length novel, *The Surprise Wedding*, they get their happily ever after. And it's wonderful. (Don't worry though, I make them stretch and work for it a bit. I mean, what fun would it be if it was all easy and glorious?)

But I won't spoil the books for you as you can experience their journey here, today, with *The Promise*, and then follow it up with *The Surprise Wedding*.

I hope you enjoy their love story as much as I do and that it makes you dream of first loves and all that can be if we have the courage to reach for it.

Happy reading,
Jean Oram
Alberta, Canada 2017

"*D*ad, nobody died." Devon Mattson sighed, trying to be patient.

"People get seriously hurt pulling those kinds of stunts," his father replied through the phone.

"They're not stunts."

Crossing the large backyard of the old, multi-bedroom house a bunch of his friends had rented just off campus, Devon waved to a few acquaintances, who shouted their congratulations on his weekend win. Tonight, music pumped from the house, overriding the usual faint sounds of the nearby Atlantic Ocean throwing itself against the shore over and over again.

"It's drag racing, Dad." Devon walked up the creaking back steps, weathered to bare wood, and entered the kitchen where the keg was set up. Most of the glassware in the high-ceilinged room sported the logos of various motor oil products, vehicle companies, or other racing-related sponsors—all earned by Devon and his racing buddies. Just this afternoon he'd brought back a case of beer steins, and he sought out the cardboard box while half listening to his father. Most of the cupboards didn't have doors and the wobbly table on the ripped linoleum floor was littered with bottles, making his search a quick one. No glasses. Didn't that figure? He raced, won, got the swag, and everyone else claimed it before he could.

He gave a mental shrug. It was all just more stuff he'd leave behind in eight months when he moved back across the continent, degree in hand. Unfortunately, that would also mean no more packages of home-baked goodies sent by his teenaged sister, Mandy, and her friend Lily. Over the past three years they'd diligently sent baking every month, something he never got when he was at home.

"Hey, how's that kid sister of mine? Any care packages on the way?"

"You can't write essays with a broken hand," his dad chided, ignoring Devon's attempt to change the subject.

"You're thinking of demolition derbies."

"At this stage of the game it would be plain dumb to get a concussion and forget everything you've learned."

"Again, more likely in a demolition derby."

"I swear you take risks just so Trish and I will worry."

Devon grinned, almost feeling bad about poking at his dad's unrelenting anxiety, which he tended to pass on to his new wife when he got really worked up about something. It couldn't be easy having all that angst eroding your happiness. "I got you thinking about something other than Mandy and Frankie, didn't I?"

His dad gave a chuckle of acknowledgment, which he cut short. "Did you hear they broke up?"

"What? Why?" The two kids were perfect for each other. Close friends who made the leap to dating.

"She says he's too much of a daredevil." His father's tone implied that the same might be said about Devon.

Sure, Devon took risks, but nothing like his sister's now ex-boyfriend who'd fallen off the water tower while painting a proclamation of his undying love on the metal tank. Apparently he hadn't heard of greeting cards or flowers.

"Sometimes the edge is a fun place to play," Devon commented as he poured beer into a plastic cup.

There was something about the grit, oil, and pure exhilaration of racing that made him feel alive and temptingly invincible, when all around him were signs that life was short, temporary and full of curve balls.

There was no sense worrying when you weren't the one in control, so you might as well go along for the ride. Especially if that ride went over a hundred miles per hour.

Devon lost track of his father's nagging as he weaved his way into the home's formerly grand salon, where at least thirty people were dancing, the music cranked up. He took a sip of beer and backed out of the room, unable to hear his father over the noise.

"Dad, I've got to go."

"Don't drink too much and don't get anyone pregnant, you hear?"

Devon smiled. "Funny, Dad." After clicking off, he slipped the phone into his back pocket and drained half his beer before heading back into the massive living room. That was the nice thing about old manor houses—they were great for parties. And even better, he got to return to his relatively clean dorm room at the end of the bash.

"You gonna go pro?" Tony asked, falling against him. His glass was embossed with the logo of today's race, Devon noted.

"You ever going to learn to hold your liquor?" he retorted as he righted his friend, who helped round out his pit crew for most races.

"Probably not," he admitted in a slurred voice. "But I keep practicing."

Devon laughed and raised his beer in a toast. "Nice glass." He continued on through the crowd, accepting high fives from friends and acquaintances as he went.

Of course he wasn't going pro. Racing was a dead end. Fun, but not what he had planned for his life.

Last summer, while working maintenance for the local mountain parks back home in Blueberry Springs, he'd been lining up a real job. If things went well over the next two semesters—and why wouldn't they?—he'd return home and walk straight into a property management position for the town.

A great job, nice community, awesome pay, and benefits, too.

Just eight months to go and he'd have it made in ways his parents never had.

He stretched muscles which were still tight from rebuilding the hilly hiking trails, and mentally prepared for two more semesters of working his brain instead of his body.

Devon paused to sip his beer and scan the roomful of familiar faces. Grease monkeys and car babes gyrated to the music. The women wore what he considered a uniform: long hair loose and free, Daisy Dukes and low-cut tank tops. It reminded him yet again why he loved the late summer South Carolina heat.

"Devon! Over here," his roommate, Turbo, hollered over the music. The man had earned his nickname due to the fact that he did everything as though he was run by a turbocharger. Whether it was talking, getting a job done, or picking up women—everything was done with speed and efficiency. The senior was into having a rowdy good time but was also an ideal roommate, seeing as he never brought parties back to their campus dorm. Not even private parties for two.

Devon raised his cup, trying to preserve the last inch of his beer as he slipped between groups of dancers. He was jostled despite his care, his cup knocked from his hand, crushed underfoot. Giving up, he let the crowd move him like a current, carrying him this way, then that. He laughed and danced, chatting briefly with people as they flowed by.

As he spun around at one point, he suddenly spotted an old Blueberry Springs friend across the room, through the mob. He was surprised she'd come to something she typically referred to as a testosterone-fueled, low-brow drunken brawl. Which was completely unfair. Brawls typically didn't happen until the wee hours of the morning and long after smart women such as Ginger had already headed home to bed.

The music was too loud for her to hear him, so, instead, he kept an eye on her in case she needed rescuing from the dude who seemed to have her loosely penned in against the bay windows. Then she laughed, and the man in question turned slightly—it was his friend Ricardo. Devon chuckled to himself. If anything, Ricardo would be the one in need of rescue, as Ginger had a thing for guys with accents and wouldn't be releasing Ricardo for some time.

Devon turned away to meet up with Turbo and just about slammed into someone. He snagged the woman and pulled her against him so they didn't topple. The silky fabric of her blouse floated between his fingers and her cascading blond hair tumbled over him as they collided. Before he could fully take her in he knew she didn't belong here, and yet somehow she felt perfect snugged in his arms. Like a piece of his world he hadn't even known had been missing.

Which was crazy.

Her big brown eyes widened as he continued to hold her, trying to figure out his reaction. Her long lashes fluttered in surprise. They stared at each other for a long moment, her hands braced against his pecs as though they'd always belonged there. As if the two of them should know each other.

Who was this woman?

"Hi," he finally said. "I'm Devon."

"Olivia," she replied breathlessly. "Do you normally embrace strangers longer than necessary?" She raised an eyebrow, politely edging out of his grasp. A flicker of amusement shimmered in her eyes, as well as something unknown and intriguing. Not quite identifiable, but definitely present.

He snapped back to the present, unsure what had come over him. "Sorry," he murmured, fully releasing her. As he did so he took in the full view of her lush curves, which were accented by her well-put-together outfit—high heels, silk blouse, diamond necklace. She obviously had money as well as poise.

She was out of his league. And out of place in the shabby house filled with adrenaline junkies spilling beer with every other move.

But man, she was something else, and he wanted to crack the mystery that seemed to have him entranced.

"No harm done," she said smoothly. She adjusted her necklace, taking him in. If his radar was working, she liked what she saw.

Ditto on that score.

"You okay?" he asked, his voice husky.

She nodded and wetted her luscious lips. "Thanks for…"

"Embracing you longer than is socially acceptable between strangers?"

She laughed before catching herself.

"Women fall for me all the time, you know," he joked, hoping to make the sun shine across her face again with another laugh.

Stupid. He was babbling, spilling trite lines, begging for attention.

Still, she rewarded him with a small smile, humoring him, and their eyes met once more. Devon didn't want to move, didn't want to lose track of her, but couldn't think of a thing to say that wouldn't sound like a pick up line.

A woman in bright lipstick and a see-through white tank top covering a black push-up bra squeezed between them, pressing her breasts against him. "You did so good today, Devvie," she purred, as she trailed a nail down his arm.

He maneuvered her to the side so he could watch Olivia. She was already escaping through the throng, her hips in those tight capris sashaying in a hypnotic way, her sleek heels avoiding the snags in the carpet. She glanced back over her shoulder, with an expression he couldn't quite decipher. If he wasn't mistaken, it almost looked like...regret.

OLIVIA CARRINGTON COULDN'T HELP but keep glancing at the man who'd bumped into her a few minutes ago. He was an exemplary specimen of deliciousness and had a check mark in every box on what she found wonderful about the opposite sex. Those sculpted muscles gave him such an irresistible allure of pent-up masculine power. He'd held her, balancing her lightly as though she didn't weigh a thing—which she most definitely did. There were no teeny designer-sample sizes in her closet, unlike in her sister's.

Olivia let her hungry gaze devour a path over the man's body, from his solid shoulders to those long, lean legs. There was something incredibly sexy about a snug white cotton tee stretched across a guy's strong build. The faded, worn jeans that hung low on his hips added to the rugged man-candy image. Pure masculinity. Add in the ease with which he moved and her imagination went straight to the bedroom.

Hello.

"Hey, princess. Like my glass?" Another guy stood in front of her, holding up a stein filled with beer.

She glanced at it, replying, "It's lovely," before trying to catch sight of Mr. Sexy again.

The woman from earlier was all over Devon, her lithe body undulating suggestively. Disgusted, Olivia turned away from the erotic sight, trying not to writhe with jealousy.

"I won it." The man went to pull up his ripped jeans, spilling some beer in the process. Olivia backed up a step to protect her Guccis and he immediately took up the space. "I'm good."

"Uh-huh." Olivia continued to edge back, trying to remain

outside his spill zone. Meeting this guy was not what she'd envisioned when she talked herself into following her roommate out tonight. She'd imagined rugged men with fast cars racing down empty streets, women cheering from the finish line. Tough men. Living on the edge.

Someone more like Devon. Olivia found herself watching the woman move over him again, the voyeuristic pull not unlike watching a car crash. She would never behave like that in public. But to have that kind of confidence, to be that bold and sexually free? It had to be liberating in ways Olivia had never experienced.

And yet despite her envy, she felt a tug of triumph as Mr. Sexy gently removed the woman from his personal space. It shouldn't matter that he didn't want another woman on him, like lace on satin. He wasn't Olivia's type, with his five o'clock shadow, shaggy hair and disregard for this season's fashions.

She sighed. It didn't matter what he wore. He was intriguing and unlike anyone she knew. Somehow he'd hooked her with just one encounter. Was it the way he'd held her, warm and strong, as if he could protect her? The way he'd made her laugh with his cheesy line?

It had to be the charm. The confidence. A complete aphrodisiac to any woman, but it shouldn't have impacted her the way it seemed to have.

"Can I get you a drink?" The man with the beer waved his glass and Olivia shook her head quickly, backing into someone behind her, one of her new heels sticking in discarded chewing gum.

"I'm fine, thank you." She crossed her wrists at her waist and tried to maintain a polite smile, looking for a way out, but managing only to back herself farther into a corner.

"Do I know you? You look familiar."

Judging from how he was gawking at her, his brain was slowly tracking back through history in an attempt to place her. Which advertisement would produce the "bingo"? A magazine mascara ad? Bus shelter lipstick campaign? Or the ever-popular TV commercials where she and her sister danced together, pretty and free, without a single care in the world?

"We probably shared a class last year," she said easily. She didn't want to talk about her family's cosmetic company and the litany of expectations that followed her around, as well as the constant nagging reminders. *Do this, don't do that. Say this, don't say that. Wear this. Suck in your gut. Don't slouch. Smile. Diet, diet, diet.*

She was at this party to try and wash away the stress of a summer filled with following their commands. Her parents still thought she'd chosen this university for its smaller class sizes and top-notch marketing management program. Little did they know she'd chosen it for the easily accessible fashion design classes. She had two more years to figure out her future before her parents expected her to graduate and continue with the image they'd groomed: the perfect, smiling daughter who showed up at all the right events, in the right outfit, with flawless makeup, and never caused a stir. The face of Carrington Cosmetics, the perfect PR rep. But with each new design class Olivia sneaked into her schedule under the guise of "it's so I understand trends," the more she knew she'd much rather design dresses than sit in an office and pretend she'd been entrusted with enough authority to influence the family business.

The man with the spilly beer was chatting on, his stale breath washing over her. Olivia clutched her tasteful diamond necklace, wishing she could escape without hurting his feelings or causing a scene.

"Hey. Olivia, right?" She glanced up to see Mr. Sexy standing beside her. "Sorry to interrupt Tony trying to convince you he's more than pit crew, but I need his help." He clapped a hand on Mr. Spilly Beer's shoulder. "Tony, my man. I can't get the keg to pour right. You know how to fix it?" He waved an empty plastic cup that was split up the sides.

There was no way he was filling that thing, but Tony swayed as he saluted him. "I'm on it, boss."

"You're a good man," Devon called after him. He turned to Olivia, his eyes soulful and sweet. "You all right?"

"Of course." She straightened her top. Did she look so out of place she needed rescuing? Talk about embarrassing. "Thank you."

"Are you here alone?" he asked, frowning as he looked around, as though seeking her reinforcements.

"Of course not. I'm here with my..." Wait. Where *had* her roommate gone?

"Boyfriend?" he asked, eyebrows raised. A riot of unexpected anticipation sizzled through her as he leaned closer so they could talk without shouting over the music.

"Roommate."

"Good. I'd hate to end up in a fight because I held you longer than was socially acceptable."

She felt a giggle attempt to escape, but held it in. Instead, she asked, "Do you do that to all the women who 'fall for you'?"

Devon had replaced Tony's physical proximity, keeping her enclosed in the corner. But unlike with Tony, she didn't want to escape, didn't feel trapped.

"Only the cute ones who like to be held for too long." The corner of his lips lifted and she laughed.

"Who says I liked it?"

He reached over to toy with a lock of her hair. "Who says you didn't?"

Olivia, unable to reply, simply bit her bottom lip and watched him through her lashes. "I think you meant to bump into me," she said finally.

"You think a man like me needs to make up opportunities to hold a woman?" He was grinning, amused.

"You're cocky."

He gave a knowing smile, not at all insulted by her observation.

"I think when you come across a woman who refuses to fall all over you, you don't know what to do."

He leaned closer, and she felt his breath against her ear. Tingles surged through her as she awaited his retort. "And would that woman be you?"

"Possibly." She trailed a finger down his chest, feeling bold. She connected with his gaze, a rush of heart-thumping excitement overwhelming her.

He caught her hand before she could break contact, his eyes darkening with interest. "So what does a man have to do to get a woman like you to fall for him?"

"Olivia!" It was Ginger McGinty, her roommate, butting in with flushed cheeks, her auburn curls a mess. "I was looking *every*where for you."

Devon released Olivia's hand and she felt the loss, the disappointment at the broken touch. She tried to school her expression, which was probably broadcasting everything to her best friend.

"Ginger, meet—"

"Devon, hey. So, Olivia, I met this guy and he offered to walk me—"

"No," both Olivia and Devon said at the same time, before sharing a quick look.

"It's not safe," Olivia stated, casting another glance at Devon. He crossed his arms, silently backing her up with a nod.

"But..." Ginger narrowed her eyes, looking from Olivia to Devon, who were standing shoulder to shoulder, like united parents ready to argue. "I didn't know you two knew each other."

How long had Olivia's roommate known this fine specimen of manhood and not said a thing? They were seriously going to have a little talk about that later.

"We *just met*," Olivia said, trying to make a point about Ginger going off with some new acquaintance.

Devon said, "She fell for me. I'm trying to convince her I'm not a god. No—" he stared at the water-stained ceiling for a second "—that I *am* a god." He winked at Olivia and she laughed. There was something about him that was just...*fun*. He didn't seem to take anything too seriously, which was a big breath of fresh air.

"So this guy—" Ginger started to say to Olivia.

"Ricardo?" Devon interjected.

"Yeah," Ginger said with a frown. "How did you know?"

How had her roommate hooked up with a man that fast? Olivia wondered. Then again, it hadn't taken her long to crush on Devon—but she wasn't letting him walk her home. At least not yet.

"I left you alone for, like, two minutes," Olivia stated.

"Ten," Devon corrected. "Ricardo's a good guy. We've been friends for years."

"But you just met him..." Olivia said to Ginger.

"Devon approves, and we grew up together." She batted her eyelashes, hands clasped in front of her.

Grew up together? Oh, Ginger was going to have all the goods on this hunk, Devon. Olivia could barely wait to hear it all.

"In Blueberry Springs," Devon explained. "Way out west."

"Plus I had classes with Ricardo last year. He's totally adorable and has the best accent." Ginger smiled meaningfully.

Olivia tipped her head to the side, staring at her friend. The woman had a soft spot for foreigners and was one day likely going to have one of those whirlwind fairy-tale romances where she woke up married.

But in the meantime she could *not* leave Olivia here. Not on her own.

Olivia had dressed down for the party, but she'd missed the

mark. Car race parties were *not* horse race parties. She stood out like a sore thumb and was well outside her comfort zone.

"What about me?" she asked. "You can't leave me here alone." Who knew how long it would take for a cab to come rescue her?

"I'll stay with you," Devon said.

"Awesome," Ginger replied with a big smile. "Thanks!" She turned, disappearing into the mob of bouncing, dancing students, who were making the floor shake along with them.

"But…"

"Looks like it's just you and me." Olivia felt the weight of Devon's arm across her shoulders, the low rumble of his voice setting her chest on fire. She wasn't sure whether she should be delighted or worried to be left alone with someone as tempting as he was.

"She ditched me."

"Ah, whatever. The whole night is ours now. We can make it whatever we want. Tabula rasa."

A Roman wax tablet, a blank slate to write upon…

That sounded tantalizing. And perfectly dangerous.

"I don't need a babysitter."

"Nobody said you do."

"So…you race?" she asked, turning to face him, while shifting out from under his arm.

He nodded. "Do you?"

She shook her head rapidly. Of course not.

"How come?"

She replied with a laugh, unable to come up with an answer that didn't make her sound stuck up or chicken.

"You like the adrenaline rush?" she asked.

"Nothing has ever made me feel as alive."

"Nothing?" she teased.

"Come with me sometime," he said, his eyes on hers. "I'll teach you." He was serious.

She couldn't imagine herself behind the wheel of a race car, but didn't want to say no and risk shutting him down. She wanted to continue the flirtatious banter.

"I'd rather you teach me how to play pool." She gave him a teasing glance, letting him know she was imagining his arms wrapped around her body as he helped her line up a shot.

He let out a bark of delighted laughter. "I like your style, Olivia."

"Want to know a secret?"

He leaned closer, a wicked glint in his eyes. His aftershave was musky, intoxicating, and she inhaled it, waiting a beat before saying, "I already know how to play."

He grinned, increasing the potent headiness of their flirting game.

"There's a diner at the end of the block," he stated.

"And?"

"Want to go for coffee?"

He thought she was drunk and needed to sober up? Ouch.

"It was nice meeting you." She went to turn away, but Devon cupped her head like he was going to bring her in for a kiss, his steady gaze making her feel seen, special.

Oh.

He didn't think she was drunk. He was interested in her.

That made her whole body feel as if a bottle of Sprite had been shaken, then let loose inside her.

"Are you going to kiss me?" she asked. "Because I'm going to kiss you."

Instead of waiting, Olivia lifted herself onto her toes and planted one on him. His lips felt unexpectedly right as he kissed her back. Gentle. Curious. Exploratory... Her arms went around his neck and an awareness filled her. This kiss wasn't just about her partner. It was about *them*. Together. An encounter powerful and sweet, full of give and take, kindness and understanding.

Her body warmed, fizzy feelings of delight working their way to her core as the kiss heated in intensity.

Olivia broke free, realizing she was in the middle of a throbbing dance party, kissing a race car driver and acting as if she was free to do whatever she wanted.

She liked it. A lot.

"Wow," she whispered against his lips. He smiled and oh, it was glorious. As though sunshine shone down on her after a lifetime of rain.

"I think I like you, Mr. Sexy."

2

*O*livia tried to distract herself from thinking about Devon and his wonderful kisses, as well as the uncharacteristic boldness that had come over her last weekend. She was embarrassed by her behavior and the way she'd likely led him on. Totally unfair of her, seeing as she would never follow through on anything beyond flirting.

Besides, they couldn't be two peas in a pod, as she'd briefly let herself believe the other night. He was fun, their teasing liberating, but it wasn't real.

She didn't know what had possessed her to act like that, but it certainly wouldn't happen again. Their lives, their worlds, were too different.

She needed to focus on reality: school, her future career in PR, and the most evil class in the history of university education, management computer systems.

Olivia had registered for the course while humoring a romantic vision of herself with her hair tucked in a bun and smart reading glasses perched on her nose as she whizzed through computer systems, printing out slick reports and graphs to take to her parents about the trends she saw unfolding in the cosmetics industry. It turned out the class produced mind-numbing frustration as she tried to keep up with the professor, who talked endlessly about computer programs, their uses, as well as project timeline breakdowns.

She'd show him a breakdown. A mental one.

The worst part was that the class had a lab portion, too. As she packed up her books after the latest lecture, Olivia decided that if sitting at a computer and clicking on the things the professor had just mentioned didn't help bring some sort of sense and relevance to the material, she'd drop the nonrequired brain bender and move on with her life. Maybe she could squeeze in another arts class without her parents twigging on to what she was actually up to—a minor in fashion design.

"Are you in the evening lab?" another student, Rod, asked, catching up with her in the hall.

Olivia shook her head. "The one in an hour."

"Too bad. We could have been partners."

She gave him a disarming smile. "Maybe next time."

"We should go out for supper. There's this great new place I've been wanting to try on the pier. Four stars." He raised his eyebrows, as though the prospect of going out with him at a romantic restaurant overlooking the nearby ocean was a temptation she'd readily succumb to. "What do you think? Tomorrow night?"

She scrambled for an excuse. They'd gone on a few dates in their first year, but once he'd seen her pull up in her Porsche he'd quickly begun "forgetting" his wallet every time, forcing her to pay as he chose more and more pricey venues for their dates. It had taken her several weeks to finally find a polite way to end things.

What if she'd led Devon on, the same way she'd inadvertently treated Rod with her wishy-washy replies?

But *had* she actually led Devon on by flirting? She'd become caught up in that feeling of harmless fun, the easy banter, but what if he'd thought it was real? Something more?

No. They were too different. He had to know that.

"Olivia?" Rod prompted.

"Oh, sorry. I can't. I'm—I'm seeing someone." The lie was out before she had time to consider it.

Rod's face fell. "Of course. Of course. Well, the offer is always open."

"Yes, thank you." She turned and hurried away before he could ask for details about her fictitious boyfriend.

Once certain she was in the clear, she slowed down, then popped into the campus café near the lab to grab herself a fancy coffee—with extra whipped cream, since there was nobody around to enforce a diet on her. Noting she still had plenty of time, she took the sunny sidewalk that stretched between buildings, slowing to skim the posters lining the various outdoor boards. Used textbooks for sale. Roommates needed. She'd sure lucked out there. Her father had bought her a cute off-campus condo along the Atlantic so she wouldn't have to deal with roomies. But she'd found it too quiet, all alone, and in her first year she'd begged Ginger, an acquaintance from her intro to management class, to come live in the spare room. The two were now fast friends and the little condo was perfect for them.

Olivia kept skimming the posters and notices, pausing abruptly when she saw one calling for wardrobe volunteers. An upcoming drama production needed five gowns designed for zombie brides.

Her heart began to thrum in her chest, just as it had when she was flirting with Devon and getting close to the do-not-cross line. The one where they'd leaned in, about to make their bodies sizzle in a we-can't-back-out-of-this kind of way. That had happened more than once in the few hours they'd spent together, their kisses heating to unprecedented levels for two people who'd just met and might not again.

Olivia drew a calming breath and shot off a text to the phone number on the poster. This was her chance to take a step toward the future she had been dreaming about. Test the waters. Prove herself.

By the time she finished her coffee and reached the computer lab, she'd received a reply, with a date and time for a meeting with the wardrobe coordinator.

The computer lab's door was still locked, so she dusted off a small spot on the floor in the narrow hallway before sitting down, feeling pleased with herself. This was going to be a whole new year, one where she seized the day and went after what she really wanted.

She glanced up as someone plunked himself on the floor beside her, and her heart began thrumming madly. It was Devon.

Oh, no.

No, no, no.

He looked even sexier today. How was that possible? She was going to flirt with him again, but take it further.

She could *not* go further. He wasn't even her type.

And that smile of his. Was it expectant?

It shouldn't be, couldn't be, but it was.

His shoulder pressed against hers and he flashed that devastating grin that made her whole body tense with anticipation. The man could have been lightning, the way he electrified her with his presence. She wanted to lift his shirt and lick his abs.

Olivia Carrington did not lick abs.

But oh, with the world as her witness, she wanted to. Badly. Really badly.

She needed to pull herself together. Be proper, careful. Safe. It wouldn't be right to have a steamy affair with a man like Devon.

Mmm. But it would be delicious.

"Hi," she said nervously.

"Hey, Libby. You in this lab?" He angled a thumb toward the closed door.

"It's Olivia," she said with a nod, disappointed that he didn't remember her name. She'd been meaningless to him. A fling that wasn't a fling.

No. That was good, she reminded herself. She didn't want to hurt his feelings or take things too far. If he couldn't recall her name, she was safe.

"Libby is short for Olivia, isn't it?"

"Livvy. And nobody calls me that."

"Except me." He shot her a grin, head tipped to the side, watching her reaction.

"Except you," she whispered, trying not to smile like someone smitten.

Oh, she was in deep.

Why did she love it so much that he'd given her a nickname? Where was her cool, unaffected poise when she needed it the most? She had to keep him at a distance so she didn't lead him on.

"Are you a management major?" he asked.

She nodded.

"Me, too. What do you plan to do with it?"

Small talk. She could handle that. Simple answers. No flirting. No innuendos. Awesome.

"Fluff stuff," she replied offhandedly. "Public relations."

"That's not fluff. It's an important aspect of marketing when it comes to brand and image maintenance."

Assuming someone let her near those kinds of decisions, yes, and didn't force her to remain nothing more than a "face" of the company, as she and her sister had been ever since they'd reached puberty.

"How about you?" she asked.

"Property management back home."

She nodded, not sure how to keep the conversation going in a way that would make her stand out, appear interesting and memorable, not a boring blank slate.

No, she reminded herself. She wanted him to *not* consider her.

Didn't she?

"Um, sorry about the other night."

"Why?" He looked genuinely curious.

"If I..." She tipped her chin upward. "If I led you on."

"Oh."

Devon waved to a few students as they drifted down the hall toward the lab, laughing and chatting.

His shoulder didn't seem to be pressing against hers as closely and she missed the connection, the touch.

"Are you good with computers?" she asked, hoping to break the suddenly awkward silence.

He shrugged. "I passed in high school. I wasn't exactly a great student." He watched their classmates mill about, his head tipped back against the wall, a small frown tugging at his lips. There was a hint of something in his expression that she couldn't quite figure out. Hurt? Regret? But she knew it wasn't those. It was something deeper. Something she couldn't identify.

Scared that she might have hurt his feelings, she tried to bring back the flirty tone she'd used at the party. "So what you're saying is that I shouldn't choose you as a project partner, since you can't help me pass?" Realizing she'd likely insulted him with her teasing, she let out a horrified squeak and quickly began apologizing.

"Were you planning on using me?" he teased.

"No! No. I'm so sorry."

"Because there are ways of using a person that are more fun than that." He waggled his eyebrows and she felt her jaw drop, horrified that their conversation was running amok.

He kept a straight face through her embarrassment before tipping his head forward, his shoulders shaking. Then he threw his head back again, letting out a laugh. His hair, a bit too long to be fashionable, flipped with his movements, and somehow it was the sexiest thing she'd seen all week.

"Obviously you're not dumb," she said tightly. "And I don't use people."

"Oh, Livvy," he said. He continued to chuckle, and she turned to face him more fully, gently pushing his forearm to make him shut up. But then became distracted by the firm, ropey muscles beneath his tanned skin. He felt amazing.

The image of ab licking came to mind once again.

Still trying to control his laughter, he dropped a hand on her knee, giving it a friendly squeeze that sent her whole body into a tizzy of hormones.

She plucked at invisible lint on her sweater, wishing she knew what to do with his hand, which was still on her knee. Was it an invitation, an expectation? Or was he just being comfortable and friendly? It was driving her nuts. She'd just *told* him they weren't…that they didn't…and now he was…

She sighed and he leaned against her, his eyes still dancing with humor.

"You look like you should be cold and boring, but you're fun, you know that, Livvy? Unexpected."

"You suck at compliments." She felt the beginning of an unwanted smile, and he squeezed her knee again.

Devon held her gaze for a moment, his eyes open and kind, and she could feel her cheeks heat in response. She could almost kid herself that he was attracted to her. Which meant there had to be something wrong with him.

Then again, she was crushing on a man who, according to Ginger, was a daredevil race car driver who'd spent the summer working with his hands. Not exactly the kind of guy she could bring home without eyebrows being raised. So maybe she was in good company, as there might be something off-kilter with her, as well.

The laboratory door swung open from the inside and she quickly grabbed her books, thankful for the distraction so she hopefully wouldn't make a fool of herself again—at least for a moment or two.

Devon hopped to his feet, extending a hand to help her up.

"I do admire a gentleman," she murmured.

He gave a playful bow. "At your service, m'lady."

As they stepped into the laboratory she pointed across the room, as though directing a naughty puppy. If they hung out together she'd inadvertently lead him on, and they'd both end up in an unwanted situation where they'd part with hard feelings. "I think you should go to the other side of the class. You're too distracting."

Devon gave her a crooked grin chock-full of mischief, one that made her want to grab him and kiss him madly. There was something about him that made her want to live, to laugh out loud, even if it meant showing all her teeth in a most unbecoming way.

He was life. Vivid and real.

"In that case," he began, moving around a row of stations, "which seat are you claiming? I'll be your partner. I can't resist a woman who falls for my charms. It's my kryptonite." He hooked her arm with his and led her forward, pointing at various stations.

She laughed, but gave in, knowing she shouldn't. But she'd warned him, right? He was an adult and made his own choices.

"This one?" he asked. "No, its chipped top will bother you. How about this one?" He stood behind the long desk, looking at the whiteboard at the front of the room. "Nope. We won't be able to see well enough. Let's move up one row."

A guy in baggy jeans slipped in front of them as they moved toward it, claiming the station before they could. Devon was approaching him when Olivia called, "Devon, this one's fine."

"I'm sorry," he said to the other student, "but my lab partner has a disability and needs this station."

"Devon!" she exclaimed, embarrassed. The closer station

would be better, but this one was okay. She scrambled forward, reaching for his arm, hoping to subtly drag him away before he caused a scene. "It's fine."

"A visual disability. She's quite sensitive about it." The harder she tugged, the faster he talked. "Refuses to wear glasses, as she fears unsuspecting bystanders will no longer be privy to the devastating impact of her chocolate eyes."

Olivia finally managed to pull him away, just as the man who'd claimed the station sighed and slid his books off the counter so he could move up one.

Devon's face creased with delight as he showcased their ill-gotten station with outspread arms. She laughed, knowing she was climbing in over her head. But the feeling was heady enough that she was willing to overlook that small fact, if it meant getting to know Devon better.

DEVON FROWNED at the systems quiz in his hand. He'd really thought he'd do better.

Then again, he'd been a bit distracted by flirting with Olivia, trying to make her laugh. She was fun, different. Plus the sexual tension between them had been building steadily since they'd become lab partners. Every lengthened look, every smile seemed to speak volumes and had his attention piqued.

And yet he knew that's all it was—just physical awareness and wanting what you couldn't have. They were from different worlds and she'd made it clear she wasn't interested in kissing him again, and hadn't intended to give him a message indicating otherwise.

Her honesty, as much as it had surprised him, also made him like her all the more.

And truthfully, he knew it would be wise to remain nothing more than lab partners, because even though they were dancing around some sizzling attraction, once he graduated they'd be going their separate ways. She'd have another year here, then would return to her family's business, where it sounded as though she was expected to marry well and continue being The Face of Carrington Cosmetics—whatever that meant.

As for himself, he was going back to Blueberry Springs, where he'd never be rich, never be able to meet her needs. He was from a family where his clothes and toys had been handed down not just to his younger brother, Ethan, but to their baby sister, Mandy. And even though his future career would be a decent one, it couldn't ever match what Olivia had grown up with.

And still he found her intriguing, beautiful and impassioned, her eyes sparkling with conviction and intelligence when she got fiery about something.

"I think we need to buckle down," he told Olivia, tapping the quiz papers against his thigh.

"Let's get a tutor."

"A tutor?" He didn't have money for that. Well, not money he *wanted* to spend that way.

"Yes." She was watching him, her blond hair tucked behind her ears. He inhaled a whiff of her intoxicating perfume. Sometimes when they studied together he could smell her on his clothes afterward, and found himself wishing he could smell her on his skin, too.

He crossed his arms. "I'll throw money at a tutor when you come drag racing with me."

She let out a laugh, but stopped when she realized he was serious. "Why?"

"Why would I spend money on that when I could just study harder?"

"Why would I take part in a high-risk activity because your marks aren't what you want them to be?"

"Because it's fun." And seeing as she'd never take him up on the offer, it was perfect. No race, no tutor.

"But it's totally unrelated. And for your information, a tutor points out what needs to be focused on, which expedites the study process. It saves time."

"Leaving more for racing." Huh. He kind of liked that idea, and the logic seemed sound. "So when are you going to take on the track?"

DEVON STILL COULDN'T QUITE BELIEVE he'd brought Olivia to the race track or that she'd agreed to come race in the first place. Remind him to never play poker with her, seeing as she'd aptly called his bluff.

Smart woman.

Now he had to hire a tutor with her. He only hoped it left him more time for the track, like she'd promised. Especially since the guys were all giving him the side eye as if he'd broken some unspoken rule. Yeah, yeah, chicks didn't hang out where engines screamed and the smell of oil and gas was prevalent. But it didn't really matter in the end, seeing as women didn't understand the need for speed, the desire to control something that was solely in your hands. Olivia was dainty and proper, so it wasn't as if she was going to come back after today. She just wanted to share a tutor to help them study better. Badly, apparently.

Devon had already taken her out in a loaned trainer car, seeing as the stock car he'd hauled out from Blueberry Springs didn't have a passenger seat. Patiently, he'd shown her how to approach the track, how to handle the car and its speed. Then they'd switched seats, putting her behind the wheel. He'd taught her when to accelerate, as well as when to brake, which was basically never. The car had gone faster and faster until she was screaming through every turn, laughing as she pulled off the entire run without incident. And then they'd raced against each other, Olivia in his car, and him in Turbo's.

He'd pulled ahead at the last second instead of letting her win, but when he met her on the tarmac she was grinning as if she'd won at NASCAR.

"That was *such* a rush," she said, tugging off her helmet. Her hair was a mess, sweat lining her brow from the Carolina's October heat, her eyes sparkling. "I can see why you love it."

"Yeah?" Devon felt surprised. "You liked it?"

"*Loved* it." She paused as though trying to put her feelings into words. "It's like I'm guzzling adrenaline as an energy drink."

He chuckled, knowing the feeling. It was incredible and habit-forming. And watching Olivia absorb the activity with such gusto, he wondered if she might truly get it.

"It's…it's like you're thumbing your nose at life," she said. "No…like you're finally free." She laughed. "It's bad-ass. Adrenaline is addictive." She gave him a playful shove. "You should have warned me."

"I didn't expect you to like it," he admitted.

"How could I not? I feel…"

"Alive?"

"Yes!" She was practically dancing with the discovery. "And invincible! Except you aren't. You could lose control at any second and that would be it. But because you're the one at the wheel, you don't die. You have your own life in your hands and nobody else gets a say."

His smile grew. How about that. Olivia, the most unexpected person, understood racing.

"I totally get my sister's collection of speeding tickets now," she continued, her face—her very body language—electric with excitement. Even in that grubby, borrowed old racing suit she looked radiant.

"I don't recommend you driving like that on city streets," he warned.

"Oh, I won't." She swung her helmet as they moved toward the air conditioned change rooms to discard their fire-retardant driving gear. She fluffed her hair and checked to make sure her diamond studs were still secured in her delicate lobes. "But I get it now—that feeling of being totally on the edge, knowing things could change in a moment, but they don't because *I* choose for them not to. Talk about power and control!"

"You want to go again?"

"Next weekend?"

"Sure."

She slipped her free hand into his, giving it a squeeze, her eyes alight with enthusiasm. Her giddiness dissipated as she met his gaze, their connection crackling with mutual need. She took a step closer, their hands still locked together.

"Thank you for bringing me here," she said softly.

Without thinking, he leaned over and dropped a kiss on her lips. She cupped his head, not allowing him to end the kiss, which started out tender, sweet. As they relaxed, enjoying the exploration, their kisses grew deeper, more insistent and probing. Weeks of teasing and holding back since the September party had punched holes in their walls of resistance and now it was crumbling, their passion and need unleashed with a fury that had Devon bracing them against the door to the change rooms, not wanting to end the kiss, come up for air or to see any inkling of doubt on Olivia's face. This felt right. More right than anything he'd ever known.

SINCE THE RACE, Olivia had spent the past several nights breathless with Devon, their mutual desire finally unleashed between the sheets. She'd never felt so alive, so free, so out of control. So connected.

He made her hungry for life and seemed to understand her frantic need, meeting it with his own, spiraling them further and further beyond the grip of restraint.

She was no longer Olivia Carrington, a face in an ad, but someone who was out there kicking butt and taking names. Living. Really living.

"Where are you off to?" she asked, making a grab for him as he tried to roll out of her bed.

He laughed and fell back against the sheets, then kissed her playfully. "Class."

"Oh, that still exists?"

He chuckled. "Yep. Come with me." He stood, reaching for her, his nude body splendid and strong and barely resistible.

She bit her bottom lip, not accepting his outstretched hand. "Maybe you should come here first." She lifted her brows and he dived back under the covers, not coming out again until they were both fully sated, but running late for their first classes of the day.

Devon brushed his lips against hers as they shared a quick shower. "You're insatiable," he said, his voice rough with desire.

"And you love it." With her eyes on his, Olivia sucked his finger into her mouth, teasing him, until he nestled her body against his and groaned. He found her rounded curves exciting and it lent strength to the feeling of empowerment she had around Devon.

"Have I mentioned that I love that you don't tell me who I'm supposed to be?" she murmured against his lips.

"And who would that be?" He cupped her buttocks, pulling her in for a deeper kiss, listening, as always, without judgment.

"I can be anyone." Everything about Devon Mattson was fun and liberating. He took each day as it came, helping her do the same, as well as helping her push back those walls her parents had used to box her in. She loved the unexpected laughter he pulled from deep within her. The way he agreed to all adventures, never judging, always opening the door of possibility.

Even while racing he'd never once doubted her ability or

advised her how to behave. He let her be. He understood. And that was the headiest aphrodisiac she'd ever found.

"Well, you're going to miss class if you don't put on some clothes." He turned off the water, his gaze drifting down her form. "Although I must say I do enjoy this look."

She giggled and stepped out of the shower, wrapping herself in a towel.

Devon rewarded her with a smile, his eyes twinkling with mischief. She could have sworn her heart sighed. She felt like a cartoon character, all dopey-eyed, with hearts circling over her head. And she was totally okay with that. He was like nobody she'd ever met. He was special.

And she'd discovered it all because she'd ventured away from the norm set out by her family. Who would have figured?

They hurried to her car, reaching it five minutes before their classes officially began. They were definitely going to be late. "I think I'll buy a race car," she said, as she put the Porsche in gear.

"And where will you park it?" Devon asked, pointedly looking back at the one parking spot she had at the condo.

"Out behind my mansion, of course."

"Right. The mansion. Which one? The one in Malibu or the one in Cape Cod?"

"I'm thinking Houston would be good for this... Maybe I'll build my own track, too."

"A smart use for your trust fund."

She smiled knowingly, playing along, even though she knew the fund in her name wouldn't be enough to set her up in the world she was describing. Plus given the way she seemed to be veering away from her family's wishes lately, that money would remain locked up when she reached the grand age of twenty-five.

"I'll need a trusty mechanic to work over my frame," she said with a wink as she turned onto the road, trying to bring Devon into the dream. "Maybe you can help me out. Rev my engine, get me warmed up."

"I might redline it a time or two," he said, his voice thick with desire. "Overheat things."

"Promises, promises," she laughed.

"I always keep mine."

"Good to know." She smiled as she parked the car, and put a little sashay in her walk as she led the way to the management lecture hall.

"I'VE GOT to help Turbo with his injection system." Devon gave Olivia a kiss, expecting she'd continue studying dress patterns for a group project at the university library and leave him to take the bus down to the track. Even though they had a tutor now—who was indeed saving him study time—he found himself spending that new free time with his girlfriend instead of on the track as he'd expected. His buddies were somewhat understanding despite their constant ribbing and his smattering of sponsors seemed happy enough, but he'd never let a woman come between him and the track before and he wanted to prove to himself that he hadn't changed his priorities.

"I'll give you a ride," Olivia said, packing up her books and papers.

"You're in the middle of things."

"My brain's fried. I need to sit and think for a bit before I start laying out the patterns."

"You sure?"

"I like the track," she said with a smile, hooking her hand in his. Her expression was so open, honest and happy he knew there was no way he'd ever say no to her. He cupped her chin, watching her for a second, enjoying his personal view of everything wonderful. He gently brushed her cheekbone with a thumb and lowered his lips to hers.

As they walked across campus to the parking lot, Olivia

chatted about her sister and how the two of them had to sit for a photo shoot on the weekend.

"Do you get paid for the shoots?"

"Paid?" She looked at him as though he'd grown an extra pair of ears.

"Yeah." He didn't think it was a strange question. He was only minor league with racing but he still had most of his costs paid for by sponsors. Why should it be different for her? She was in fashion magazine ads.

She shook her head. "It's for family. The business."

"So then can you model for anyone?"

"Nobody else has ever asked." She leaned against his arm, her lips downturned, then brightened falsely. "Tell me about your siblings. I know Mandy loves to bake. Any more brownies come your way lately?"

He laughed, knowing Olivia was now just as hooked on Mandy's delicious brownies and care packages as he was. "No more baking due for another few weeks."

"You have a brother, too, right?"

Devon nodded, thinking about Ethan. His brother was in deep with a woman Devon wasn't sure felt the same level of interest.

"What's wrong?" Olivia asked.

"You know you're a distraction?" He kissed her, loving how she lit up every time their lips touched. "I should drop management systems and retake it next semester. I bet my marks would improve dramatically."

"You missed the drop date, so you're stuck with me, buster." She pretended to sock him in the arm. "And I know you're pulling straight Bs and will probably bump that up to an A now that we have a tutor."

He laughed, knowing he was caught.

"So what's up with your brother?"

Devon shrugged. "He's fine."

"Oh, you're going to go all silent. Brooding. Love that."

"You really want to know?" he asked, facing her car, his back to her.

"I do."

"Fine. He's going to propose to his girlfriend and I think she's going to say no."

Olivia's arms slipped around his waist from behind, hugging him. "And you're worried about him?"

"A bit." Although he'd never admit that to anyone else.

She scooted around so she was facing him. "That's sweet."

He tried to push out of her embrace, but she held him tight. He watched her for a moment. She was everything. Kind and sweet, but tough and cool, too. "You're a walking contradiction."

"You're trying to distract me so I don't realize how gooey and sweet you are on the inside."

"My—our—parents are divorced, and I don't want to see him go through that pain. That's all."

"Who says his marriage would end in divorce?"

"She doesn't love him."

"You're thinking of saying something to him?"

Devon gave a brief nod.

"Don't."

"What? Why not?" He felt himself begin to get lost in her gaze. That pleasant quicksand where he'd slide in, deeper and deeper, unable and unwilling to break out. For a split second he thought that he might be doing the same thing Ethan was. Falling deeply for someone who, quite possibly, would never feel the same. In fact, what were he and Olivia expecting out of their current relationship? Were they serious? Was it simply a fling? Sampling a snippet of a different world—one they'd never live in?

"People get married for reasons other than undying love," she said softly. "And maybe she loves him just as much as he loves her. If you say something and you're wrong, then what?"

"And if I don't, then what?"

33

"It's his life."

"But I'm his brother."

Olivia suddenly dropped her arms, no longer holding him. "You're family, but you don't get to decide his life."

"I'm not trying to—"

"Devon. Don't interfere." She suddenly looked fierce.

"So I say nothing?"

She simply gave him a look.

"You're probably right," he said, pushing a hand through his hair. "He loves her right to her core and always will. No matter what life throws at them and how they change, he'll always love her. It's the one thing that can't be erased."

"Are you a romantic, Devon Mattson?" Olivia teased.

He gazed at her in surprise. "You don't believe in love like that?"

"I prefer being a realist." She gave him one of those flirty looks down her nose that he adored, half hoity-toity and half playful. A ruthless combo where his attraction was concerned. "But..." she took a breath "...when I get married it's going to be for love. And that man had better love me back just as strongly."

"Fist bump to that," Devon said, holding out his clenched hand so she could bump hers against it.

"Throw me in the loony bin if I ever marry for money or social standing, like my parents did." She made a face and stuck out her tongue.

"I'll sweep in on a white horse and drag you away if need be."

Olivia laughed and let them into her car. "Riding up on a white horse might just get you tossed in the psych ward, too."

"As long as you're there with me, it'll all be worth it."

OLIVIA FOLLOWED Devon into the pits at the race track, seeking his roommate. He didn't seem to be anywhere, despite a crew saying they'd seen him just a few minutes ago.

"Think we missed him?" she asked, taking Devon by the hand.

He shrugged, his brow furrowed. "Let's check the prep room."

Feeling playful, she raced up to the award podium, which had been pushed to the side of one of the lesser used pits, standing on the top platform as if she'd just won a race. She beamed at Devon, pretending he was the audience, then blew kisses and thanked her sponsors before leaping into his arms. He caught her, holding her tight, kissing her until the nearby track's lingering scents of gasoline and car exhaust vanished, the sounds of growling engines and peeling rubber forgotten. It was just them on the cracked asphalt.

Slowly he released her. "You make me forget what I'm doing."

"Likewise."

"What *are* we doing?"

"What do you mean?" She felt something big coming and slipped from his grip.

"Have you told your family about us?"

"Well...no. Not really." They wouldn't understand. The way she felt around Devon, inspired, happy. Like she was living a true life...

"Where are we going, Livvy? For real. Are we just playing or is this something bigger than that?"

She wound her arms around her waist. "My parents aren't... they wouldn't understand."

"Wouldn't understand or wouldn't approve?"

Olivia reached out to touch his arm. "Devon, I—"

"Devon," a man called from one of the tunnels that led out of the pit area. "Turbo's looking for you as is one of your sponsors." The man cast Olivia a look she could best describe as unwelcoming.

Devon began pulling Olivia along, but she broke free outside a washroom.

"I'll catch up in a minute." She gave him a smile, knowing it would be better if he arrived without her and was able to start playing the hero before she appeared—hopefully, after he'd disarmed his friends. If they were happy with him, they'd be happier with her, because even though she didn't know where their relationship was going, she wanted his friends to like her.

"We'll be down the hall," Devon said. "Or on the other side." He placed his fingers to his lips, then to hers, hesitating as he gave her a look so simmering with affection she thought it might be love. Before she could confirm it, he hurried away with his friend. Olivia took a deep breath to quell the need that had begun to build inside her like an avalanche ready to let go, and stepped into the washroom.

She fluffed her hair, reapplied her lip gloss, then went looking for her boyfriend. Just as she reached the gate at the end of the hall that led to one of the tracks, she heard a familiar voice. She paused, trying to place it.

"Man, she can't be serious about you. Not long term."

Olivia stopped, head cocked. It didn't sound like Devon, but it could be Turbo. Who was he talking about?

"Dude, whatever." *That* was Devon, his voice devoid of his usual humor. She froze, feeling exposed. They were talking about *her?* Devon was being warned off?

"Look at her. Look at you."

Olivia unconsciously glanced down at her designer jeans, her bright new sneakers. Devon had come in ripped jeans of a brand she'd never heard of, and a tattered pair of Converse she figured he kept for sentimental reasons. But maybe it was more than that. She knew he was putting himself through college, which wasn't a small financial feat for most.

It didn't matter, though. She didn't care that they came from different economic backgrounds. She liked him. A lot.

Devon laughed, his voice filled with affection as he said, "I know. She's something, huh?" She could practically envision him pushing a hand through his hair, with that delighted look that made his eyes shine whenever he was reminded that she'd chosen him. It was the exact same way she felt.

And that feeling would get them past any bumps, such as friends who doubted their compatibility. She quietly checked the gate to see if it would open, wanting to slip to Devon's side, silently back him up.

"She's nice and all," the man said, "but you're gonna get hurt when she goes back to Richie Rich Land."

"Thanks for your concern, but we're fine."

"Where were you today?"

"Studying."

"With her?"

"Of course. We share a class."

"Your sponsors are going to drop you if you don't start acting more serious about racing."

"I'm leaving stock cars in less than a year."

There was the sound of tinkering, metal on metal.

"Who wears diamonds to the track, Devon? She's not from this league."

Olivia's fingers flew to her understated studs and she backed against the wall. She wanted to run, hide.

"I like her." Devon's voice was hard. "She gets me. You like who you like, and the rest is just details."

Olivia felt the same way, but was it enough? He'd asked her earlier if she'd mentioned him to her family. She hadn't.

Why?

Because it would be this same conversation, but in reverse. She didn't fit in here, just like Devon wouldn't fit in with her parents. He was part of her current world, which was separate from the one her parents were setting up for her.

She liked having Devon in her life. She knew that. But did that mean it was time to take a stand and speak out for what she wanted, as Devon just had with his friends?

You like who you like.

Olivia backtracked down the hall, trying to sort out her mind and her feelings.

By the time Devon caught up with her again she was composed. She took one look at him and that open, loving smile of his and knew somewhere along the line their desire and friendship had turned into something deeper, stronger, more compelling.

Something she needed in her world no matter where she ended up.

"Come to the gala with me," she blurted out.

"Gala?"

"It's not for a few weeks, but my family will be there. Come meet them."

"As your date? I don't think that's a good idea."

"Why not?"

"I'm pretty sure your parents would see me as an act of rebellion."

"Is this because of what your friend was just saying?"

Devon looked surprised that she'd eavesdropped, but didn't pursue it. Instead, he said, "It's pretty clear we're from different worlds."

"I care about you."

"I care about you, too, but it doesn't mean we need to go swiping at hornets' nests."

"Are you afraid? Because I've never felt more whole or more content in my entire life than I have since being with you. You're part of my life, Devon."

3

*D*evon straightened the cuffs on the tuxedo he'd rented for the night's gala fundraiser sponsored by Carrington Cosmetics. He wasn't sure what to expect and only hoped he wouldn't embarrass himself or Olivia. He *had* to make a good impression tonight.

If he failed he might as well kiss their relationship goodbye, seeing as Olivia was obviously wound up about how her parents would take their friendship. Because even though she said the right words, she had become anxiety incarnate, and the closer they'd crept to the night of the gala, the more reserved she'd become, proving to him that her folks held the cards a little more firmly than she'd led him to believe.

As he let himself out of his dorm, laughing off the catcalls from his buddies, he mentally reviewed the collection of etiquette tips Olivia had been slipping in here and there over the past week as her nervousness grew. As much as he'd been kidding himself that their relationship was merely about burning off their attraction, it had become something much more addictive. Much more consuming and meaningful. For both of them.

He had to make tonight work. He had to dazzle and shine,

because he'd rather jump in front of a stock car going at top speed than allow her to be crushed by his failings.

Devon's phone rang as he left campus to meet Olivia at her condo. It was his brother, Ethan.

"Did you ask her?" Devon asked without preamble.

"Chickened out."

Devon sighed. It wasn't the first time Ethan had summoned up the courage to ask Dani to marry him, and had then backed out. Maybe somewhere deep down inside, his brother feared his relationship ending like their parents' had.

Devon understood those doubts. The fear. The suspicion that at some point, no matter how deeply you felt, that you might end up like his mother had with Devon's dad—you and your love simply wasn't enough.

Occasionally those doubts sneaked in, attempting to steal the joy he felt around Olivia, to overwhelm what they had with expectations for the future. But over the past few weeks, each passing day had only added layer upon layer to their growing relationship, making it stronger and tighter than anything he'd ever experienced.

He was in deep and he'd be kidding himself if he said he hadn't fallen in love. He wanted to fit into her life so fully, entwine so deeply, that they no longer knew where their individual lives started and ended.

Which, again, meant he needed to ace tonight.

As he ended the call with his brother, having joked around until Ethan got out of his funk, Olivia came to the door of her condo, looking resplendent in a long gown that swirled around her like a dream. Every curve he'd come to know and adore was showcased by the stunning design. It was as though the designer was in love with her form as much as Devon was, and wanted to show it off.

It made him want to whisk his girlfriend away, make love to her all night. That and hide her from every hot-blooded male on the continent. And maybe also have a little chat with the expert seamstress Olivia and her designer friend had hired to put together their creation. But truthfully, he wasn't sure if he'd compliment everyone profusely or ask them not to assist in creating any more earth-shattering, mouthwatering garments for his girlfriend.

"I saw you arrive," she said, closing her house keys inside her beaded clutch. "Did Ethan propose?"

Devon shook his head, not wanting to dwell on his brother's floundering love life when he had a gorgeous woman of his own in front of him. "You're beautiful." He bowed, placing a light kiss on the back of her hand, when chaste was the last thing he wanted to be. "I'm going to be fighting men off you tonight."

Olivia blushed and swatted him away. "You're too much."

"I'm barely enough." He couldn't seem to rip his attention away from her. She had done something with the makeup around her eyes, giving her a savvy catlike appearance. It made him think of the time she'd prowled her way up the bedding, his roommate away, a sly look in her eyes before they'd rocked the bed frame into the wall. So much for claiming his security deposit when he moved out.

Her hand still in his, he swept it toward his mouth, planting another kiss upon it.

"If you keep devouring me with your gaze I'm going to get ideas," she whispered.

"We could go inside?" He glanced at her building, but she shook her head.

"Ginger has a group project."

"Then I hear coat closets are a good place." He gave her a wink.

She laughed, her anxiety from earlier in the day obviously back in full force. "Don't even tease! We have to be so good and so sweet tonight our heads are going to ache."

"I have a good remedy—gin."

"Chardonnay would be even better."

"Well then, if you insist, m'lady, I will wait until midnight to be naughty. But then you are all mine." Devon wrapped an arm around her waist, his cheesy act dropping as he drew her into a kiss. His duty tonight was to be perfect, meet her parents' expectations and settle Olivia's nerves about pleasing them.

"You always make me feel wanted and beautiful," she whispered after another kiss.

"Because you are."

"We're going to be okay tonight, right?"

He gazed at her, seeing a hint of vulnerability—the real woman beneath the polished exterior and impeccable manners. She was like him, occasionally lost within herself, unable to see outside of it all. He hugged her tight, letting her know she wasn't alone.

"We'll always be all right, Liv."

Her hands slipped inside his tux jacket, weaving a pattern along his back he now equated with her feeling frisky. Their kisses turned deeper, hungry.

The autumn night was crisp and quiet, and he leaned them against the oak that shaded the door of her condo. Olivia, head tipped against the bark, panted as his lips roamed lower, exploring the bounty of cleavage exposed.

"Livvy, baby, we need to head inside," he murmured at last.

She suddenly pulled her wrap higher on her shoulders, pushing him away, her anxiety returning. "No. We can't be late."

"Hmm. So you're saying arriving late with you looking thoroughly sexed isn't the best way to make a good impression tonight?" he teased.

She shuddered with nerves and shook her head, not reacting to his joke.

Devon swallowed hard and wondered what level of hell he was about to step into.

OLIVIA STRUGGLED with a deluge of mixed feeling about the gala which was located close to her hometown up the coast, hours from campus. Part of her was in its element among the elegance. She knew what to expect, what to say, how to act. Second nature. Another part despised the stifling, stuck-up world of expectations and all it represented.

Covering her nervousness with a demure smile, she approached her mother, who was holding court near the stage where a charity auction would be occurring in an hour.

The earlier certainty that had prompted Olivia to extend the invitation to Devon dissolved as her mother's cool glance took her in with one quick sweep. Then made a slightly longer sweep over Devon, who was standing beside her.

"Darling." Her mother kissed her on both cheeks, her attention then moving to Devon. "I don't believe we've met. You are...?"

"Devon Mattson. Pleasure to make your acquaintance." He shook her mother's hand with a precision Olivia had exacted out of him on the way over. And despite his rented tuxedo—which actually looked quite dashing on him—Olivia thought he might fool a few people. At least for a moment or two, and hopefully long enough that they might give him a chance.

"I'm sorry," her mother said, "I don't believe I've met your parents. Are they from around here?"

"Mother..." Olivia jumped in, feeling her mom's disapproval pressing in like a cold wall in a storage locker. "Devon is from the small town of Blueberry Springs. Devon, this is my mother, Mrs. Joan Carrington."

Olivia held out the skirt of her cream dress, wanting to hear what her mother thought of her pattern-making group project. She and Adele had spent hours poring over the design before entrusting it to their professor—a retired designer—who'd brought the one-dimensional plan to life as part of the class. The feedback and criticism on the pattern's flaws, as well as the constant design tweaks, had been hard to take at times, but she felt the final product made her shine, and she was eager to show it off.

"What do you think?" she asked. "In my—"

"Olivia, dear," her father said, planting a dry kiss on Olivia's temple as he joined them. "You're looking well. Have you smiled for the photographer yet?"

"No, not yet."

"Make sure you and Emma get a photo together. A nice one. We'll use it for next year's marketing."

"Daddy? I'd like you to meet Devon Mattson." Her hands trembled as she made the introductions.

Devon remained stoic as her father gave his hand a brief shake after giving him a once-over. "Nice to meet you." He turned to face his wife, Olivia's date not seeming to make it onto his radar. "Joan, I heard the Brownstones want to make a sizable donation. Can you take care of them?"

Her mother smiled. "Of course." She began scanning the room for the couple in question, waving when she caught their eye. Before she moved away to join them, she grasped Olivia by the arm. "I told Luke to save his first dance for you."

"But…" Olivia's gaze flicked to her boyfriend. She'd told her parents she was bringing someone when she'd arranged for the extra ticket. How could they so blatantly discount him? Overlook him, when he was standing right there?

Her mother slipped away, smiling at the approaching couple that was always happy to add an extra zero or two at the end of their donation figure. "Sophia, so wonderful to see you. Is this the gown you picked up in Paris?"

"Who's Luke?" Devon whispered, leaning close to Olivia's ear.

"I'm so sorry. He's an old family friend." She felt caught, and hoped he'd understand her obligation to play nicely.

"How old?" Devon raised his brows, making her smile despite the anxiety swelling inside her.

"He's a few years older than us." Handsome, kind and from a wealthy family, but there were no sparks between the two of them. Still, that didn't seem to prevent their families from trying to set them up with each other.

"Ah." Devon nodded, getting the picture. He wasn't smiling, and she wondered if it had been a mistake bringing him here, if the way she had to jump through hoops would hurt his feelings.

She felt someone standing behind her, and realized the small orchestra had begun playing. Swallowing hard, she turned to face Luke.

"May I have the honor of the first dance?" he asked, his blue eyes smiling at her.

Automatically, she placed her hand in his, even as she tried to excuse herself. "I am actually—"

Before she could finish her sentence he was sweeping her into his arms, their feet falling into the practiced steps drilled into them from an early age. She glanced back at Devon, feeling as though she was betraying him, abandoning him.

Cameras flashed around them as the dance floor filled with other couples, and her mother caught her eye, tipping her head in displeasure as she mouthed *"Smile!"*

Olivia immediately complied. Luke was chatting while he moved her around the ballroom. She knew they looked striking together—they always seemed to make the society news column, along with a photo, whenever they met up—but she still didn't feel that spark she used to hope for.

"How are classes?"

"Oh, fine." She paused before remembering her manners. "Thank you."

"I'm helping my father relaunch his skin care line."

Before she'd met Devon she'd half believed that one day she would end up married to Luke Cohen, merging their two family companies. He was one of those men where you could end up married and it would be all right.

But she knew now that "falling into marriage" wasn't even in the same universe as what she had with Devon.

"We should go out on my boat next spring. Sail around Kiawah, have lunch. Maybe slip out to do a little kayaking or enjoy a round of golf? What do you say?"

The idea of a romantic trip around the popular sea island just south of Charleston on the boat of one of the most eligible bachelors was something that would have made the old Olivia smile, feel special and chosen. But now there was only one man who could make her feel that way and it, unfortunately for Luke, wasn't him.

"It's difficult to make plans so far in advance. I'm not sure what my class schedule will be like," she hedged, as the song wound down. "Thank you for the dance."

She took a moment to collect herself as she searched for Devon. He wasn't where she'd left him, and she was worried he might have come to the wrong conclusion about her based on her family and the gala and had gone home despite not having a ride.

"Olivia! Mother looks so amazingly bothered by your date." It was her sister, looking completely tickled by their mother's foul mood. "The obedient daughter isn't so pliant tonight." Emma did a saucy shoulder shimmy, her moxie level at full bore.

"Emma..." she warned. Her sister had to go home with their upset parents, and Olivia bet they'd be even more bothered if they found out she'd just blown off Luke and his invitation.

She sighed, feeling the weight of her family's expectations press down on her from all sides.

"Smile!" a photographer exclaimed, holding his large camera up in front of the sisters. They fell into position out of ingrained habit, heads tipped together, smiling sweetly. The photographer moved on after snapping his shot, and they resumed their conversation as though they hadn't been interrupted.

"Way to stick it to Mom and Dad." Emma seemed unable to stop grinning.

"He's not some game, Em. He's my boyfriend."

Olivia found Devon in the crowd and started toward him, her sister following her gaze as she trailed along.

"He's hot."

It was more than that, Olivia realized. His steamy looks may have initially drawn her to him, but she'd since come to know him, she found herself more amazed by the way she felt so alive whenever they were together. It felt as though everything would be okay as long as she was with him.

"You're in love with him!" Emma exclaimed, clapping her hands over her mouth as though suddenly privy to the most sordid gossip in town. Her eyes lit up with the joy of knowing someone else was going to cause a crisis at the dinner table for once. Although Emma, despite all the hassle she got from their parents, somehow always managed to toe the line well enough that her speeding tickets and other exploits never quite made it into the major gossip circles.

Around them, people turned to look at Emma, and Olivia batted her sister's hands away from her face, hushing her. "Shh!"

"You are!"

"Would it be so bad if I was?"

"But he's…"

"Don't say it," Olivia begged. She just needed everybody to go away, to settle down. She hadn't brought Devon here in order to rock the boat, and it felt as if things were quickly going to be blown out of proportion.

"Everyone is talking about him, you know."

Olivia's gaze drifted to Devon, who was holding two glasses of chardonnay and drifting their way. Someone tried to take one from him, obviously thinking he was a waiter.

It was like the guy at the race track had said. *Look at her. Look at you.* Everyone could tell how different they were with just one glance, even though she'd bought him the right haircut, the right pair of shoes.

It wasn't fair. And it wasn't right.

And she was powerless to change it.

Devon caught her eye and smiled, but afraid he would misinterpret what was surely showing in her expression, she turned back to her sister. Olivia struggled to hold in every ounce of emotion that was threatening to come spilling out. She'd been stupid to think her family would see the changes in her. That they would respect them and allow her to follow her heart.

"What's wrong?" Emma asked, suddenly concerned.

"Pray you'll never understand."

DEVON WAS WALKING TOO FAST for Olivia, but he couldn't seem to slow himself down as his stiff, fancy shoes ate up the boardwalk along the edge of the ocean.

He didn't belong in her life.

He'd been a spectacle, someone to gossip about.

That part he'd expected and could handle. The part he couldn't handle was feeling as if he didn't know the Olivia who had been in the ballroom, smiling and allowing her family to push her off on another man.

Olivia. The woman he loved.

He had no idea how they were ever going to make up the distance that stretched out between them tonight. For the past month and a half, had she really been doing as Turbo suspected—using their relationship as a way to distance herself from that sterile, judgmental life in an act of rebellion?

He'd known how important her parents' approval was to her, but tonight had given him an all new view of just how much she hated to disappoint them. How much Devon and Olivia's life differences could pull them apart. How badly she could betray him.

"Devon," she panted. "Slow down."

He'd left the ballroom without a word. He'd taken one look at Olivia's expression after her dance with Luke, while she was talking with a woman he'd assumed must be her sister. He'd caught Olivia sizing him up before she turned away, cold and unemotional, and it had been enough.

He'd already noticed the looks he'd gathered in the glitzy ballroom, the slow taking in of his rented tuxedo, of being overlooked or treated like staff.

He didn't belong. But it hurt to have her turn her back because of it.

"Devon! Please."

He slowed, turning to see The Face of Carrington Cosmetics under one of the antique-looking streetlights that lit up the boardwalk. An older woman had stopped Olivia and her sister at one point, placing a palm against each girl's cheek, taking them in as though they were an object or novelty, instead of two human beings with lives and dreams. Olivia had simply stood there and smiled, as if it was normal to be treated that way.

And maybe it was.

But if so, it was just another example of how different the two of them were.

"What was that in there?" he asked, keeping his voice low and seemingly unaffected.

"Hopefully, they won't notice we took off, or they'll kill me."

"You didn't have to leave."

"I came with *you*, Devon." She gave him a pointed look, as if her statement was supposed to make him feel better.

He knew tonight hadn't been easy for her, either, but he'd still expected more from her, expected her to be stronger. Knowing she'd left because of him and was likely to suffer the wrath of others should appease him, but he was still having a difficult time letting go of his anger.

"Promise me that if I ever let my parents choose my groom, you'll throw me into the ocean," Olivia said sourly. She kicked off her high heels and strode off the lit up boardwalk and down to the dimly lit ocean's edge. She stopped just before the waterline and stared out across the choppy sea. The woman who had been ablaze with happiness only hours ago was now deflated and glum, and he felt partly to blame for not trying harder. He just hadn't expected to be judged so quickly and harshly, and then to be discarded so carelessly. He already knew he would never make up for whatever failing her parents and friends had seen in him tonight, leaving him at a loss about what to do, how to move forward.

"How is this going to work?" he asked quietly, coming up behind Olivia. If they stayed together they'd face these kinds of events over and over, and there was no way he could handle her rejecting him like that again—intentionally or otherwise.

"You're supposed to ride up on your white horse to rescue me from the wrong groom, the wrong life, remember?" she replied, her voice wobbling horribly.

They stood for a long moment, the sound of the dark and brooding ocean crashing in upon itself filling the air.

"What was that in there?" he asked again.

"Which part? The part where I was expected to be a pretty face and do everything Mommy and Daddy asked, or the part where I exploded on the inside because everyone was so judgmental?"

The harshness in her voice was unexpected.

"I think that...about sums it up."

"I'm so sorry. You must have thought I'd lost my mind." She gently touched his forearm before tapping herself on the forehead and exclaiming, "I acted like a—like a robot! Falling into the old habit of smiling and acting like it's all good. It wasn't. And I'm sorry if you felt...felt like you were..."

"Like I was less than?"

She nodded, her bottom lip tucked tightly between her teeth, her eyes glittering with remorse.

Devon stared out at the rolling waves, trying to sort out his feelings. "I didn't belong in there," he said at last.

"Neither did I." She turned to him, her dress's skirt bunched tight in her fists. "I'm sorry. I thought it would be better."

"Are galas always like that?"

"I'm disappointed to admit that they usually are."

He reached over to rub a bit of lipstick that had smeared at the side of her mouth.

"How long has it been like that?" she asked, dolefully.

"Not long."

She sighed. "Like they don't have enough to chastise me about already."

"They're going to talk about your lipstick?"

"Carrington Cosmetics? They've only recently entrusted me with the ability to apply my own makeup for events like this."

"Hard-core."

"What am I going to do? They'll never see me for who I really am. My mom didn't even notice my dress." She smacked the skirt in frustration.

"These things take time." He lightly ran a finger between her brows, chasing away the tension that had settled there. Olivia leaned against him, and he wrapped his arm around her waist after a second's hesitation, securing her against him. Sheltering her.

Her voice trembled as she clung to him. "I don't know how I'd survive if I didn't have you." She slipped her head out from under his and gazed up into his eyes.

His heart ached. "You looked like you were having fun." Until after the dance, when she'd realized who she'd be stuck with for the rest of the night: him.

The sting was still there, but already wasn't quite as bad as earlier. Odd as it was, seeing her pain helped.

Olivia's eyes shone with unshed tears. "It wasn't fun." Her face scrunched in pain and he pulled her closer, alarmed at her sudden vulnerability, tucking her head against his tux again. He rocked her and shushed her sobs, surprised at how one small event had knocked her down.

"Sorry if I made it harder for you."

"No," she said fiercely, her eyes wet as she pulled her head away from his chest. "It's not you. They didn't even..." She sniffed, fighting another bout of tears.

Still holding her, he drew one of her hands against his heart, then after a pause, lifted it to his mouth, placing a kiss along her knuckles. It was something he used to think cheesy, but now found irresistible and tender.

As much as tonight had sucked, Devon couldn't imagine his life without her—the Olivia he'd come to know outside the gala.

He opened his mouth to speak, but she silenced him by placing a finger over his lips. He savored the touch, feeling the weight of the universe as he became lost in the depths of her gaze.

"They are the ones who have it wrong, not us," she said softly. She pressed a hand against his chest to emphasize her coming words. "I love you, Devon."

Suddenly, the weight constricting him was gone, and Devon was filled with happiness. His Olivia was the true one. Not the one inside playacting the debutante. And because of that, they were going to be okay.

This was real.

"I love you, too," he whispered.

"I know this is complicated right now, but I need you in my life," she said. "I can be myself around you. I don't have to act or pretend. I *like* myself when I'm with you. Stay with me, even though tonight made me look like a fool." She was holding his shirt in a tight grip, her brown eyes pleading with him.

"We'll find a way, Liv."

"Promise?"

"I swear on my white horse."

She laughed, her earlier worries and tensions vanishing. "I love you so much."

He smiled back, knowing they'd figure it out.

Because at the end of the night only one thing mattered: the most beautiful woman at the gala was going home with him tonight, and she loved him with a fierceness that rivaled his own.

4

*D*evon rolled onto his side, stretching and yawning. The tutor had given them a review sheet that was kicking his butt.

Olivia was stretched out on the other side of her bed, frowning over something she was sewing.

"That for the play?" he asked.

She held out a long piece of satin covered in sequins and beads. "It's supposed to be a belt for one of the gowns." She rubbed her eyes before stabbing at another bead. "Remind me again why I'm making these by hand?"

He smiled, knowing that despite her doubts and grumblings, she had the money to buy her way out of the problem should she want to. And after the gala and the resulting pressure from her parents to conform, he was pleased to see her sticking with it. Choosing this life and not retreating back into pleasing her parents at every turn might mean there was still room for him. That there might be a chance to merge their worlds somehow.

"They're going to be beautiful."

"And look like a hack made them." She groaned and fell back

on the bed, her hair cascading around her. "The lady at the retirement center made it look so easy. Just stitch, stitch, stitch."

"That's cool that you found someone to teach you the technique."

"Yeah, it is." She sighed and lifted her work in front of her. "I told my parents I was volunteering." She dropped the belt and stared at the ceiling.

"You lied?"

"Well, technically it is volunteering, since I sit and visit with my lovely old ladies."

"Are you going to stay back at Thanksgiving and finish the costumes?" The play would open the night after Devon's last exam, which was coming up fast. They had less than a week of classes before the Thanksgiving break, which was followed by hell week where everything came due followed by exams. Just thinking about that lineup of stress coming his way had him reaching for his cup of coffee and chugging half of it.

"No, I'll still go," she said, rolling onto her front to contemplate her sewing. She stopped and looked up, sticking out her tongue. "I have to appease my parents."

"They're still upset, huh?" It had been weeks, but Olivia and he had barely talked about it, neither of them having a solution to the problem of their different worlds, and expectations for what life would be like after they'd graduated.

"They did not like me leaving early."

"I should apologize."

"You, shush." They'd been over this before. He felt he should own up for causing her to leave early, but she said her parents would use that as a strike against him, not as a mark proving his character.

They were at an impasse and he wasn't sure how they'd ever manage to sway her parents into accepting him. Likely it was a dead end.

"I don't want to damage the relationship between you and your parents."

"Lucky for you, there isn't one." She concentrated on her sewing, her brow furrowed.

He let her work in silence for a moment before saying, "I guess you going away for a few days is good. Fewer study distractions." He gave her a wink, which she returned with a sly smile.

"If you flunk you'll get to spend another year here with me." She batted her eyes and he chuckled, leaning over to kiss her.

"Right, and have even more student loan debt. Thanks, but no thanks, Liv."

She wrinkled her nose. "Being here and doing the long-distance thing is going to suck. I don't want to give up a single minute with you."

"I feel the same." He leaned back against the headboard and she moved to snuggle against him.

In five months they'd be faced with trying to find a way to balance their lives and lifestyles, but until that day came he planned to enjoy every minute they had together in their little university world.

"You know there's a bridal store in Blueberry Springs?" he said.

"Ginger's grandma's store. What about it?" Olivia turned her head to look at him.

He shrugged, his attention caught by the belt she was working on. "That's good, you know. So was your dress."

"I had help. And I've had help with this, too."

He watched her, wondering if there was a chance, even a small one, that she'd come to Blueberry Springs with him after she graduated. Work her way into a job designing dresses for Ginger's grandmother, Wanda. It wasn't a far stretch to think she could do it.

Her breath was brushing his cheek, sending rivulets of desire through him.

"If you stay back over Thanksgiving I can do more Christmas shopping for you." She tapped his chest, smiling.

"I thought you were done?" Ginger had hinted that Olivia had bought him something expensive, and had suggested he add a few zeroes to his budget or get creative.

"I just want to spoil you, that's all," she said.

Devon studied her for a moment. He worried that the disparity in their gifts would highlight the differences in their worlds in a way they couldn't avoid seeing once again.

"I can't spoil you, Olivia."

"Hon," she said, rolling onto her knees to face him. "It's not about the money."

That's what people with money always said.

"But I can't give you what you deserve."

She watched him for a long moment, taking him in. "Maybe I want things only you can give me, Devon."

DEVON MADE everything look and feel easy when Olivia was around him. Except for getting her mind to settle on management systems. Not when the last beaded belt for the drama costumes was just about complete and sitting within reach.

She sighed and flipped a few pages in her textbook, searching for an easy spot to jump in. Every page made her feel she was heading down the wrong path. But, she reminded herself, if she went into design she'd still need these management skills. And she'd also need a backup plan in case the money didn't come rolling in—which also entailed this management degree.

Picking at her chipped polish, she made a mental note to get her nails redone before heading home for the break, wondering if she was truly considering leaving Carrington Cosmetics. How would she do that without being disowned? She knew there was no way she could pursue design jobs while doing PR for the company.

Even though she'd ignored Devon's hints that she could work for Wanda, Ginger's grandmother, in his hometown, she loved the idea. But not yet. Olivia wasn't ready to upset the status quo by walking away from her family obligations and expectations. She needed a bigger springboard, as she knew her parents would accept her decision to pursue a different career only if it would shine a brighter light on the Carringtons.

Because everything she did reflected on them. If she left the business—their own daughter denying their life—and her designs flopped, well, the press would have a field day with that. She had no option but to succeed. Spectacularly.

She watched Devon frown over his notes as he went back to memorizing material. She was going to miss him when she went home tomorrow night, and it felt like all they'd done this week was study. It was good her marks were at an all-time high, but she was tired and wanted to hang out with her boyfriend. Without textbooks interfering.

"Let's take a study break." She made a grab for Devon, but he rolled out of the way on her queen-size bed, where they had their books and notes laid out. She pulled herself onto all fours, launching herself at him. They were studying here because she had a private bedroom and a big bed. He did not. *Hello?*

He laughed and kissed her. "We have to learn this stuff, Livvy."

"Ugh. Systems are *so* boring. Kissing you is much more fun."

"I agree." He plucked a cookie from the care package his teenaged sister and her wannabe chef friend, Lily, had baked and mailed. Olivia swiped a mini brownie for herself, popping it into her mouth.

"Mmm. These are delicious. Move them away from me or I'll gain the freshman fifteen all over again." Okay, the pounds she'd gained in her first year was a bit more than fifteen and her mother, as a result, had put her on a strict veggie-filled diet the following summer. Olivia pushed the box of treats away before reaching over to draw a finger down Devon's chest. "How do you stay so fit with all these care packages?"

He shrugged and winked. "I have a girlfriend who helps me work it all off."

She bit her bottom lip in anticipation, her body aching for him. If he didn't help her burn off the desire, she'd find herself in the condo's community pool doing laps—her fallback way of dealing with stress when Devon wasn't available.

"My flight's tomorrow," she said. "I'm going to be gone for days." She rolled onto her back so her hair was spread across his textbook, her gaze locked with his. She smiled coyly. "Can I tempt you into a break yet?"

His eyes drifted down her body and he leaned over her, his lips meeting hers before he licked and nipped his way down to her neck.

Lately it felt as if their worlds kept colliding, her own confusion about what she wanted to do with her future smacking up against everything else. The two of them connected so well she sometimes forgot how different their lives actually were. But then, when they were together, nothing else mattered.

She wound her legs around his as their kisses continued to heat up.

"Did I ever tell you I love it when my bed smells like you after you leave?"

She felt his lips curve into a smile on her neck and she arched her spine, encouraging him to move lower. She could just about envision what it would be like to have everything in her world smell like him.

5

"*D*id you see this?" Olivia asked, happily waving the play's program in front of Devon. Her name was listed under Costumes. Listed as a contributor, and not because of her family's money or any association with them. She had earned it, and she had done it on her own.

Devon smiled, shifting so he could sling an arm across the back of her chair, his knees pressed against hers. His fingers stroked her shoulder and he looked at her with such pride she could barely breathe. "Good work, Liv."

She smiled at the nickname and snuggled closer.

"I can't wait to see them come onstage." The wardrobe coordinator had allowed her to sneak out to watch the curtain open, but had requested she come backstage afterward to be on hand in case any of the actors had wardrobe malfunctions.

Across the aisle and a few seats down, Ginger was sitting with someone new. The thing between her and Ricardo had been like a polyester fire. Hot and quick. And yet Ginger had already moved on, because nothing seemed to get the woman down.

"The costumes were a lot of work," Devon said supportively.

"I'm going to spend my whole Christmas break sleeping."

He smiled and gave her shoulder a squeeze.

She was going to miss him while in the Caribbean with her family. The easy banter and teasing flirtatiousness. Among other things, of course.

Over Thanksgiving she'd told her sister she was designing the dresses for tonight, and Emma had said it sounded dreadfully boring. They'd ended up fighting about the fact that Emma was *happy* with the life their parents had set out for the two of them. Olivia had asked her, "Don't you ever want to do something? Something of your own? *Earn* something?"

Her sister had rolled her eyes and laughed, replying, "Daddy's loaded. I'll never have to earn a thing."

Olivia couldn't understand it. The life her parents wanted her to live was colorless compared to what she'd found with Devon. How could her sister want that? Sure, it wasn't going to be smooth sailing, as she and Devon hadn't quite figured out what to do when he graduated in spring. But she knew they'd figure something out. They were in love. Love always found a way.

She turned toward the stage again, impatient for her debut as a designer. Settling deeper into the theater seat, she mulled over the past few months. Her new life felt like it was pulling together, slowly, surely. She still didn't know how she was going to convince her parents to let her follow this path, but she had hopes that they would eventually see she was living a life that excited her, impassioned her, and that a big part of that was due to Devon and his unfailing support.

She leaned closer and whispered, "I love you."

He responded with a kiss, one finger hooked beneath her chin. "I love you, too." His eyes locked with hers and she felt such a tremendous flood of well-being and contentment.

"I wish we could spend Christmas together."

"Me, too," he said with a smile. "Did I tell you my brother is going to try proposing to Dani again? Christmas Eve."

The theater curtains began to open and Olivia popped upright. "Shh! It's starting!"

She was nervous and excited, and didn't know whether to squeal and watch every second of the play, or to run and hide and ask for a summary later.

She peeked over at Devon. He was relaxed, not a worry on his mind. She needed to channel his laid-back attitude. He was good at going with the flow, but at the moment she wished he didn't look so at ease. Didn't he know how nerve-racking this was? If he was stressing out, then she could be the one to chill out for once. Or at least chill in comparison.

The play began and Devon grasped her hand, beaming at her as the zombie brides entered the stage.

They looked incredible! Real.

She'd done that. She'd made it happen.

For the first time in her life, Olivia felt as though she had it all.

OLIVIA ROLLED ONTO HER BACK, letting the sun bite her exposed skin. All week she'd felt sick with loneliness, from the moment she'd open her eyes until she'd finally manage to wash her faraway boyfriend from her mind.

She yawned and stared up at the palm fronds above her, realizing just how much she'd changed over the past four months. Last month, at Thanksgiving, she'd been busy catching up with friends, and hadn't spent much time around her family. But now she was stuck with them for three long, dreadfully painful, unbuffered weeks. Her parents were judgmental, unforgiving, entitled, snobbish and condescending.

That was nothing new. However, her hope that they would understand her desire to follow a career in design was waning with each day she spent poolside with them.

"Do you still feel ill?" her mother asked, taking the lounger beside her. "You look pale."

"It must have been that chicken." She knew it wasn't anything she'd eaten, but try explaining longing to her cool, unfeeling parents.

They sat in silence for a few minutes, her mother flipping through a fashion magazine.

"Mom? How do you think those designers got their start?" Was it easy? Did their families believe they were crazy for taking the risk and trying?

"Hmm?" Her mother flipped up her oversize sunglasses, tuning in to Olivia once again. "Most of them create such horrid things just to get a reaction." She held up a page showing a rail-thin model in a tattered dress that no woman in her right mind would wear. At least not with that over-the-top makeup and scarecrow hair.

"They're making a statement," Olivia said, quoting one of her professors. "Shaking up the establishment."

Her mother gave the model another critical glance before letting out a disapproving harrumph and turning the page.

Olivia rolled onto her front again, adjusting her chair, unable to find a comfortable position.

She propped herself up on her elbows, watching people play in the pool. Two teenagers were splashing and flirting, looking for excuses to touch each other. They reminded her of Devon, and she looked away as another wave of nausea worked its way through her. It seemed her ache for him was getting worse, not better.

Emma joined them, standing in Olivia's sunshine. "Wanna swim?"

"Want to," their mother corrected.

"You're blocking the sun," Olivia complained. Her sister took a step to the left.

"Let's swim." Emma dropped her cover-up, revealing a

string bikini that was on the tiny side, showcasing more of her breasts than it covered. Her sister was sexy. Perfect. Her life easy.

Olivia shaded her eyes, looking up at Emma as she shook her head. "No, thanks."

"Why are you so mopey?" Emma pouted, throwing herself on the lounger beside Olivia.

"I don't feel well."

"I haven't seen you so down since Mom took away your nail scissors so you'd stop cutting the lace off your party dresses."

"Poufy lace skirts are a horrid way to try and mask a chubby kid."

"Big boned, sweetie," her mother said, not looking up from her magazine. "And those dresses were adorable and very expensive. They were designed by Louie Ree."

Emma and Olivia shared a look.

"Come swim. It'll make you feel better," Emma begged.

Olivia shook her head. "The water's cold."

"It's perfect."

Her mother closed her magazine, setting it down beside her. "There is something wrong with you." She stood, wiggling her fingers at Olivia. "Come. We'll get the resort doctor to sort you out. We didn't bring you all this way so you could be ill the entire time."

Reluctantly, Olivia followed her, hoping the doctor could find a way to explain to her mother that she was simply a woman in love.

DEVON STARED AT HIS PHONE. Olivia wasn't coming back to school. She was transferring. Leaving.

He rubbed his eyes and reread the text. The message didn't change and it still didn't make sense.

No matter how long he puzzled over it, he couldn't figure it out.

Something had to be wrong. He had to find a way to speak to her in person, to understand.

He paced his dorm room, tapping the phone against his lips. He stopped, began to type a reply, then backspaced until it was gone. He resumed pacing, thinking.

He knew Olivia. This wasn't like her. She loved it here and didn't want to be anywhere else.

When he'd texted her a few days ago, saying Dani had said yes to Ethan's proposal, her reply had lacked the enthusiasm he'd expected. He knew her family had been insistent that she'd been fighting a bug, but she'd said she'd only been tired and missing him. Now he worried it was something bigger—especially if she wasn't coming back.

Was she sick?

She wouldn't transfer if she was, would she?

He called Ginger, Olivia's roommate, hoping to gather some helpful hints.

"Ginger, what happened to Livvy? Is she okay?"

"She's here packing. The movers are coming Wednesday," Ginger said quietly. "She told me not to tell you, but something's wrong, Devon. I don't like it."

Devon rubbed his eyes with his free hand, unable to sort out the sudden change. The two of them shared every thought, hope, fear and dream. And now Olivia was in town, but hadn't told him? What did it mean, other than she was obviously shoving him out of her life and didn't want a confrontation?

"I'm coming over." Devon slipped into his shoes.

"Her dad is here," Ginger said quickly.

"Why?"

"He's acting like a guard dog," she said hesitantly.

"Why?"

"I don't know. They're talking about her transferring to a

different school, but I get the feeling she's dropping out." Ginger's voice shook with what he figured was fear for her friend.

What had changed, that Olivia was avoiding him, and her father was now taking over her life? Had she told him about wanting to pursue design, and as a result he was kiboshing her chosen school so he could keep a better eye on her? That seemed unnecessarily harsh and controlling.

She had to be sick. Was she not telling him because she wanted to protect him from the worry and pain of whatever she was going through?

That didn't seem right, either.

"Can you distract him so I can talk to Olivia? Alone?"

There was a long pause. "Give me five minutes. When you see us leave, you'll have maybe fifteen… My health plan won't cover an actual trip to the hospital."

Devon flew down his dorm's stairwell. "I don't know what you're planning, but remind me to buy you a beer. Or three."

"Take care of her, Devon. Make sure she's okay."

"I promised to always be there for her, Ginger. It's not something I plan on breaking. Ever."

OLIVIA SLOWLY PACKED clothes into a suitcase, leaving most of what was in her room for the movers. She tipped her phone toward her. Still no reply from Devon about her transferring schools. She hesitated, then picked up her cell, ready to dial his number.

She glanced down the hall of the condo and saw that her father was furiously typing on his laptop, with a force that would likely void the computer's reasonable-wear-and-tear warranty. The coast was momentarily clear.

Olivia wiped her eyes and let out a long sigh. What was she going to say to Devon? She needed to talk to him, but didn't know how he could help, how he could fix this. Bringing him in would only make it messier. It would be best to let him know in a month, after her parents had settled down a notch or two and a real plan was in place.

Placing her phone on her bureau, she sucked in a slow breath, steadying her emotions. She'd failed everyone. Disappointed her parents. Ruined her future and was in the process of breaking her boyfriend's heart.

And that was only the beginning.

"Oh! Oh, I think I need stitches!" Ginger appeared in the bedroom doorway, her face pale, her eyes darting. She was clasping a tea towel around her left hand.

"Ginger!" Olivia hurried to her side, just as her friend loosened the towel enough to show a flash of red. So bright. Olivia flinched and leaned away. "Daddy!" she cried. She covered her mouth, a bout of nausea rising fast and furious at the sight of Ginger's awful injury.

Her father appeared in the doorway, looking clearly annoyed at being interrupted from completing his work.

"Can you take Ginger to the hospital?" she asked, fighting the urge to lose her lunch. "She cut herself."

Her father took one look at Olivia and drew Ginger away. "You stay here and pack," he instructed.

He began guiding her friend down the hall, but just before they turned the corner to the front entry, Ginger glanced back and gave Olivia a knowing wink. Moments after they left the condo, the front door opened again. Olivia knew exactly who it was before he could appear around the corner and pull her into his arms.

DEVON'S HEART was beating hard and fast in his chest as he held Olivia close. "Are you okay?" he asked.

Her body, which felt so good, so real pressed to his, tightened. "I'm pregnant."

Devon went cold with shock as the knowledge slowly seeped in, flooring him. "But we were careful."

How many men had numbly uttered those exact same words?

"But I know nothing is a hundred percent," he added quickly. "It's just...I'm just...I'm surprised."

Pregnant.

A baby.

That explained it. And changed absolutely everything.

Panic began to rear up like a wild horse within him, and he sought a place to sit down as Olivia eased out of his grasp. He settled for a little table, its contents clanking and clattering as the furniture struggled beneath his weight. Devon tried to think his way through the shock, and felt another tidal wave of panic build inside him. An overwhelming, pulse-pounding freak-out, where he'd never manage to get himself reined in.

They weren't ready for a baby.

A short-term illness, maybe. But a family?

That was lifelong.

Stunning.

He drew a hand across his jaw. He needed to fix this. Do the right thing. Make it all okay for Olivia.

But he couldn't think of a single thing to say. Not even a joke to lighten the tension that was currently blocking his ability to breathe, to think, to process.

Why hadn't he thought of a baby? Why had he assumed an illness? A baby was better.

Joy. Life.

But a baby was huge. Life-altering. Entirely scary, in a way he'd never considered before.

Olivia wouldn't look at him, and it felt as though she was putting distance between them, as she had at the gala. She was standing, back straight, appearing proper and composed. But to someone who knew her? She looked entirely wrecked.

He'd done that to her.

Taken her life and turned it upside down, in probably the worst possible way.

She was leaving. Going to hide away. Without him.

"You don't want me to..." He couldn't figure out how to phrase his fears, give voice to them, without making them become real. He waited for her next words, his mind racing ahead, trying to fathom how a baby meant their love no longer had the power it did a few weeks ago.

"Abortion isn't an option, and I can't hide the baby while I'm here..." Her voice broke, her face creased, her stress evident.

"We'll figure this out," he said, his voice low.

"We already have."

"We have?"

"My parents..."

Devon felt as though he'd been slapped. Her parents would take her away, shut him out, prevent him from having a voice, a say. That was not happening. Olivia and the baby were his.

"You and I—we're not ready for this," she said, her voice controlled and remote.

"So what?" The icy-cold dread was returning, slowing down everything in his world as his brain settled in on the truth behind her words.

Deep down, he'd known Olivia was out of his league, that things were going to be tricky. But he'd never once thought he'd hear her speak this way, to deny him so blatantly and intentionally.

He tried to ignore the pain, his continuing shock, knowing she had to be scared beyond belief. He needed to be calm, put his own emotions to the side, protect her. Use logic. Reason. Come up with something better than what was already arranged.

They loved each other. That had to count for something. Something big.

"I'm graduating in four months. I'll be walking into a great job with benefits. We'll have more than most people have." He clenched and unclenched his fists. They could do this. They could figure it out. They had to. "I have family in Blueberry Springs."

"You don't understand."

"Then help me understand." He was a storm of panic and anger as he grabbed her hands, trying to cling to their thinning connection. Her fingers were stone cold, trembling. "Let me be a part of this."

"You don't understand what I've done to my family." She was avoiding meeting his eyes, and it felt as though she had knifed him between the ribs.

He wasn't enough. He had sensed it hovering out there on the horizon since the day they'd met, but hadn't noticed it coming in on him so fast, hadn't expected it to hit so hard.

"We had plans, Livvy. You were going to design dresses. We can still do that."

"Devon, that was a stupid, childish dream." Her eyes were flashing as she retreated, pulling away. "I have to be able to make a living. I'm an adult, and I've done adult things with adult consequences."

"Come to Blueberry Springs with me."

"So I can be unwed and pregnant? With no career? No degree? Like this hasn't been shameful enough for my family." She pulled her hands from his, holding them out as if to keep him at bay. "I can't do that to them. I'll go away. Have the baby." She paused and swallowed hard. "Then I'll...I'll pick up what's left of my life and carry on. I suggest you do the same."

She couldn't possibly think that was the best option, considering the blistering passion they'd shared over the past few months. Their relationship was special. They had created something magical. It was theirs.

"We love each other, Liv. That hasn't changed."

"Can't you see? It's not enough, Devon." She crossed her arms across her cashmere sweater. "People *plan* these things!"

"But I love you."

"I've already decided, Devon. I've failed myself, my family, you. It's disgraceful, and I won't talk about this anymore."

"Stay here. Marry me."

SHE WAS GOING TO FOLD. Olivia could feel her resolve weakening with every ray of hope, every lifeline Devon threw her way.

But the cold disappointment from her parents... An unrelenting wave of nausea reminded her of who she was, where the two of them had ended up. She couldn't marry Devon. Couldn't live in that dream world they'd naively believed in over the past few months. Things weren't going to be okay. They weren't going to work out. Not with something this big.

"Please understand. This isn't what Carringtons do. I've hurt my parents enough and I need to make this right."

"Marry me." He stepped closer, and she began shaking her head at his insistence.

"I can't."

"Because your mom and dad won't give you permission?" His face was dark with anger, and unlike anything she'd seen from him. "Because suddenly they have more choice and voice than I do over my own child, over the woman I love?"

"They want you to give up your parental rights."

"Like. Hell." He was leaning forward, his face pale, but full of fight.

To argue with him would drain her of the last bit of resolve and strength she'd shored up within herself. She wanted to remember them happy and in love. Not like this.

"When I'm around you I believe I can fly." She chose her words carefully as the tears fell. "I can't fly, Devon. I screwed up and you need to let me fix this."

"This isn't a Livvy problem, it's a you-and-me problem. Nobody else's."

"I'm not strong enough," she said, her voice harsh.

He swallowed hard, his own pain so clear and present it made her want to lash out. She was the one in trouble! Not him, whose life was simple, easy. He didn't have to change a thing. He could just walk away.

Olivia would have given up everything to be with him. But Devon consumed her. Encouraged her to believe in fairy tales. Following him into life led to too much loss, and she couldn't take it.

"I promise to stand by you, to be there."

"If you want to be there for me, you need to leave. Let me deal with this. Alone."

"No, with your mommy and daddy," he corrected.

"They know what to do." They were calm, unemotional. They knew how to get her life, her world, back on track again with minimal upset.

"Was everything you said just a big lie?" Devon snapped. "Now that it's no longer perfect, you're running back to the very people you said were out to destroy your soul?" He took a step back, as though disgusted with her. "I can't believe you're willing to just roll over and give up."

Olivia held in a sob.

Devon stared at her for a long moment, his expression hard and unforgiving. "You were using me."

"Devon, no. You have to understand," she pleaded.

"You were using me to upset your parents. You never planned

to choose a life with me. Well, I hope it worked. I hope you get exactly what you want out of this. Is the baby even real?"

"Devon, I didn't lie! It's not like that. *Please* believe me."

He simply stood there, shaking his head, as though he couldn't believe how she'd betrayed him, when all she was trying to do was protect them both.

"If you love me," she said, her voice wobbling, "let me do what's best."

He stormed to the door and flung it open. Ginger, looking sheepish, stood on the step, her hand washed of its fake blood. She gave a feeble wave as Olivia's father stomped toward the condo in a rage.

Devon ignored him, turning to face Olivia. "Call me when the baby's born and I'll give it a loving home." He paused half a beat before driving in the knife. "Because I know what love is."

Olivia threw herself against his arm, discarding her pride, pleading with him to understand. "I'm not strong enough, Devon. Please. This is the only way. You have to believe me."

"I thought I knew you," he said, his tone so cold it made her flinch. "I believed you when you said I was enough, that you loved me. I was a fool, Olivia, but I won't be again."

6

*D*evon stared at his textbook, unable to concentrate. He needed to take a shower, but Turbo was using it. Devon shucked his sweaty tee, leaving him in socks and a pair of running shorts.

He'd begun running after Olivia told him the news. He'd walked out of her condo, his feet moving of their own accord, faster and faster, fueled by his anger. He hadn't stopped until he was miles out of town. He felt like Forrest Gump, but he understood the character's compulsion to just run and never stop.

If he stopped he'd have to try and make sense of things.

That had been more than a week ago. Nine and a half long days of being alone with his anger, and he hadn't heard a word from Olivia. He knew he'd been cruel, cold and hurtful—just like her. But he'd been serious about being the baby's father, and he worried that things would happen without him. That he'd lose his child, as well as Olivia.

His phone buzzed with a text and he looked at the screen. Ginger. She'd talked to Liv again.

He dialed his old friend, not wanting to miss even a nuance

through the wonders of text messaging. He wanted the full story with every bit of truth, unfiltered.

"You talked to her? Will she sign over the rights to the baby yet?"

"Well, hello to you, too, Devon. How's the new semester going?" Devon growled and Ginger laughed. "Everything's fine and it's been her first morning without sickness, so yay!"

Devon checked his watch. It was almost suppertime. Ginger had been sitting on information all day and hadn't called?

"She says she's working on her parents."

"What do you mean?" he asked quickly.

"They're pushing for a closed adoption—"

"I know." Devon refrained from cursing, knowing he had to be patient if he wanted things to work in his favor. But Ginger had already told him that two days ago, as well as slipped in enough details to give him hope. False hope, he suspected. But that slim shred of brightness still taunted him at the end of his long, dark tunnel of day-to-day existence.

"She's working on them not disowning her if she gives her parental rights to you."

Devon felt the vise that had been squeezing his chest let go. He snatched up a small purchase he'd made, holding it like a talisman.

"Thank you," he said. He needed to study hard, go home, start working, start planning for becoming a dad. It wasn't going to be easy, but he wasn't giving up on that child. He'd made a promise to be there for Olivia, and in his mind that promise extended to their baby.

"Devon?"

"Yeah?"

"Just…don't get your hopes up. In case."

"Right. Thanks." He clicked off the phone, squeezing the chill out of the tiny gift in his hand, knowing he was a fool for having bought it, for selling his stock car. It was crazy what hope could do to a man, even when he was broken and angry.

Before he could collect his thoughts and get back to studying, his phone rang out a familiar tune.

He answered before it could ring again. "Liv?" He knew he sounded desperate, but didn't care.

Her voice was shaking. "It's over."

"What is?" Cold dread seeped through him. "Livvy, where are you?" He grabbed the key to Turbo's motorcycle and headed for the door, knowing instinctively that she needed someone by her side.

"I had spotting. The doctor's say it's gone."

"The baby's okay?" He placed a hand against his chest in relief, then paused. *Shirt.* He wasn't wearing a shirt. He returned to his bedroom to find one.

"No, Devon." Her voice had an unfamiliar hardness. "*It's* gone."

He sank to the floor as comprehension slipped in. In his fist he held a dream. A dream that had dissolved to dust.

"Why didn't you call me sooner?" he whispered. He could have been there. Despite the miles, he would have found a way to be at her side, to get there in time.

"You don't have to worry about being a dad anymore," she said, her voice bitter as she ended the call.

Gone.

Devon remained in a daze on the floor until the sky outside his window became streaked with orange from the setting sun.

Gone.

He pinched the bridge of his nose and let out a shaky breath.

Everything was gone.

Olivia. Their relationship. Their family. Everything he'd poured his heart and soul into over the past few months. His joy. His everything.

With his free hand, he grabbed a textbook and threw it

against the wall, then pressed the heels of his hands against his eyes, his fingers still trapping the token against his flesh.

A man didn't have someone like Olivia walk into his life and then leave him unchanged, undamaged, when she left. It was the kind of love a guy never got over, and Devon wasn't sure how he'd ever be able to stand again, be able to carry on.

His hand ached, and he realized he was still clutching the gift for Olivia. He slowly released his fingers, dropping it to the floor. It rolled once, before tumbling onto its side, taunting him. A diamond solitaire.

EPILOGUE

*D*evon blinked at his vibrating phone. This was the third time it had interrupted him while he was trying to write an essay on effective leadership. He'd promised himself no breaks until he had a rough draft. As much as he wanted it to be, he knew it wasn't Olivia calling. It would never be Olivia.

But what if it was?

It would be a long time before he'd be able to stop loving her. More than once he'd considered transferring to her new school—Harvard business, in a seat secured by her father. Now that she was free of Devon and the baby, Mr. Carrington had situated her in a cushy lifestyle once again. Devon had also considered simply dropping out, finishing his degree online or somewhere closer to home. But he'd stayed, unable to face the real truth: Livvy wasn't coming back.

He hadn't listened to his friends. He'd been burned, and he needed to accept that.

Devon needed to hobble through his last few months of classes. Return home to Blueberry Springs and try to pick up the pieces of his empty life, shards so sharp and jagged he wasn't sure he could ever piece them back together again.

"Hello?" he snapped, finally picking up the phone. It was a number he didn't know, local to Blueberry Springs. It had better not be his father calling from somewhere other than home so he'd pick up so he could nag him about his marks again.

"It's Ethan," said a small female voice, choked with tears.

"Mandy?" His seventeen-year-old sister was crying, sending him into alarm mode. "What happened? Where are you? Whose phone are you on?"

"I'm at the hospital. He—he had an accident."

Devon's mind began ripping through worst-case scenarios and he had to sit down.

"The doctors think it's b-bad. He hasn't woken up and they think he might be p-paralyzed."

Devon cursed under his breath, his chest aching. "Where's Mom? Dad? Trish?" he asked, his voice tight. Whose house were his siblings supposed to be at this week?

"Mom won't stop staring at the wall and Dad keeps freaking out. Trish can barely calm him down. I'm so scared." Mandy's voice had gone low, hollow.

There was nobody there for his sister, nobody strong enough to defuse the geyser of pain that had spewed up among them. They needed someone to pull them together.

But Devon didn't feel he could be that man. He was already gutted, angry. Not someone who could be at the helm in a crisis.

He couldn't stand any more loss. Any more pain.

"Where's Dani?"

"She won't come to the hospital."

Devon had known she wasn't good enough for Ethan. That his brother was more invested than his fiancée was. Apparently it was a trait that ran deep in their family.

Devon laughed bitterly to himself and glanced around his room. The place was devoid of anything that mattered to him, and he realized with surprise that he was, in fact, the perfect

79

person to help the family, as he was too ensconced in his own emotional drama to lend any turmoil to the new one.

His mind made up, Devon thrust a pile of shirts into a travel bag with enough force that they came tumbling out the other side as the stitching gave way. Cursing, he threw the bag aside and dug out a backpack.

He began packing again, wondering if he'd ever find his way back to this dorm and the hopes he'd had for his future.

What would be the point?

There wasn't one. Not now.

He grabbed another stack of shirts, and a ring box tumbled to the floor. He picked up the velvet-covered container, slowly flipping it open.

Diamond ring.

A solitaire. Solitary. Just like him.

Devon had to sit again as a heavy weight of grief crushed his lungs.

"Devon?" asked his sister. She was still on the other end of the nearly forgotten phone.

"Yeah. Yeah, I'm still here, Mandy. But I'm coming home. Tonight."

He stood, zipping his bag shut, after dropping the ring box inside.

WHAT'S NEXT?

FIND OUT WHAT HAPPENS TO DEVON AND OLIVIA IN THE SURPRISE WEDDING!

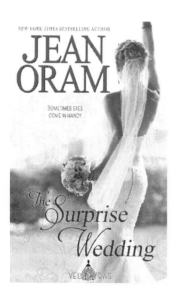

Book 1: The Surprise Wedding.

Find out what happens to these two lovers when they meet up ten years later. Will Devon forgive Olivia? Find out!

Because sometimes exes come in handy!

VEILS AND VOWS

Find love in unexpected places with these sweet marriage of convenience romances.

The Promise (Book 0: Devon & Olivia)

The Surprise Wedding (Book 1: Devon & Olivia)

A Pinch of Commitment (Book 2: Ethan & Lily)

The Wedding Plan (Book 3: Luke & Emma)

Accidentally Married (Book 4: Burke & Jill)

The Marriage Pledge (Book 5: Moe & Amy)

Mail Order Soulmate (Book 6: Zach & Catherine)

ALSO BY JEAN ORAM

Have you fallen in love with Blueberry Springs? Catch up with your friends and their adventures...

Book 1: Whiskey and Gumdrops (Mandy & Frankie)

Book 2: Rum and Raindrops (Jen & Rob)

Book 3: Eggnog and Candy Canes (Katie & Nash)

Book 4: Sweet Treats (3 short stories—Mandy, Amber, & Nicola)

Book 5: Vodka and Chocolate Drops (Amber & Scott)

Book 6: Tequila and Candy Drops (Nicola & Todd)

Companion Novel: Champagne and Lemon Drops (Beth & Oz)

THE SUMMER SISTERS

Taming billionaires has never been so *sweet*.

Falling for billionaires has never been so sweet.

* Available in paperback & ebook & audio! *

One cottage. Four sisters. And four billionaires who will sweep them off their feet.

Falling for the Movie Star

Falling for the Boss

Falling for the Single Dad

Falling for the Bodyguard

Falling for the Firefighter

ABOUT THE AUTHOR

 Jean Oram is a *New York Times* and *USA Today* bestselling romance author. Inspiration for her small town series came from her own upbringing on the Canadian prairies. Although, so far, none of her characters have grown up in an old schoolhouse or worked on a bee farm. Jean still lives on the prairie with her husband, two kids, and big shaggy dog where she can be found out playing in the snow or hiking.

Become an Official Fan:
www.facebook.com/groups/jeanoramfans
Newsletter: www.jeanoram.com/FREEBOOK
Twitter: www.twitter.com/jeanoram
Instagram: www.instagram.com/author_jeanoram
Facebook: www.facebook.com/JeanOramAuthor
Website & blog: www.jeanoram.com

Made in the USA
Middletown, DE
21 August 2021

45791577R00057